Sanguine Sincerity

BY

Eidahs

COVER ART BY

KEMVEE

BINKY INK

THE LITERARY ARM OF BINKY PRODUCTIONS

WWW.BINKYPRODUCTIONS.COM/SANGUINESINCERITY

Published in 2024 by Binky Ink
Cover & Portrait Art by Kemvee

ISBN: 978-0-09919965-8-2

<u>**WARNINGS:**</u>

Strong Language, Mature Sexual Subject Matter,

Violence, Blood, Smoking, Marijuana.

Sanguine Sincerity is the first of an ongoing series of
Supernatural LGBTQ Erotic Romance Thriller books.

Sanguine Sincerity
LIAM DONAHUE

Sanguine Sincerity
JULIAN LALLARD

Table of Contents

<u>PROLOGUE</u>

Six months before present day.

The colourful lights in the club blazed and flashed as clubbers danced to the blaring music. Clad in his favourite tight black jeans and open V top, Liam bent down to pick up a box of lemons. He hefted the box onto a shoulder and started towards the other end of the long counter.

'Excuse me,' came a voice behind him, 'are you Liam?'

'I most certainly am!' Liam gave a small wave as he continued towards the far end of the bar, focused on his task.

'Are you a bus boy, a bartender?' the other man shouted to be heard over the music.

'Bus boy some nights, bartender others, and tonight,' Liam placed the box on the counter, 'I'll be whatever you need me to be.'

He finally turned to face the man speaking to him, only to stare into the most captivating eyes he had ever seen, and Liam's heart skipped a beat. Smiling from the other side of the counter, the man's pale face glowed the various colours of the neon lights. A mild line of black eye shadow around his eyes made their blue seem even brighter. He wore a black leather jacket over his shirt and a smile that made Liam nearly swoon on the spot. Liam's gaze darted to the man's lips, redder than his own, where the alluring smile beckoned his racing heart.

'Well then, it seems you are to be my trainer tonight.' The man held out his hand. 'I'm Julian, the new guy.'

'Oh, welcome to Nightly Glow Club,' replied Liam, shaking the man's hand. His skin was soft, and Julian continued to hold Liam's hand even after they were done shaking.

'And perhaps once my shift ends, you can be my date?'

Liam's heart leapt. 'Wow, diving right in,' Liam said with a timid laugh. He couldn't help but feel relieved at the invite, after having felt such a fierce flutter from just looking at the guy. People usually could tell right away Liam was gay, but Julian could have been any other straight guy.

'I dare to be bold when I see a man who's caught my eye.' A flicker of doubt crossed Julian's porcelain face. 'Please tell me you're into men and I haven't just made a fool of myself.' He self-consciously let go of

Liam's hand – where his fingers had touched, his warmth remained. 'I apologise if you're not, I just . . .'

The two stared at each other. Julian's black hair waved near the ears and his eyes grew earnest. Liam's smile widened, and with his opposite hand, he shyly tucked his long sun blond bangs behind his ear. 'You're all right. I'm gay.'

Julian let out a relieved laugh. 'Glad to hear it.' He bit his lower lip nervously and Liam's stomach did something he'd never quite felt before.

'Right then,' said Liam, snapping back into focus and grabbing one of the lemons. 'Lemon wedges.'

* * *

After his shift, Julian helped Liam clean up since they worked till closing. As they walked along the corridor that led to the club's backdoor, Julian turned to Liam.

'Everything's closed right now but I'm still hoping you can be my date.'

Liam felt his cheeks grow warm; he felt giddy. He locked the big steel door and turned to Julian. 'I wasn't certain how serious you'd been before.'

'Why?' Julian asked, his voice tender. 'Have other men dared to ask you out only to forget about it later?' They chuckled.

'You're different from most other guys I've met or been with,' observed Liam.

'I confirm that I am,' replied Julian. He looked up at the summer sky that sparkled with stars. 'The moon is getting low. Dawn's still a little time away, though.'

'You a stargazer or something?' inquired Liam.

'Or something.' Julian looked around. 'You know, here works. I mean, it's not the most romantic spot but . . . I'd like to get to know you.'

'Well, I'm Liam, I'm twenty-four, and single.' Liam grinned timidly.

Julian laughed. 'I'm Julian, twenty-eight, and single.' He shook his head, blushing. 'You're very . . .' He smiled nervously and looked at his feet, biting his lip again. 'I don't know, the minute I saw you I just . . .' He trailed off.

'Yeah, I know what you mean.'

Julian laughed self-consciously again. 'This has never happened before.'

'What, walk into a club to spend the next hour cutting lemon wedges?' joked Liam, as he leaned back against the brick wall.

Julian breathed out a laugh. 'Walk into a club and find myself mesmerised by the most vivid green eyes on the most handsome face I've seen in . . . years.'

Liam felt his stomach whoop. He and Julian stared into each other's eyes, smiling flirtatiously, and continued their chat until Julian looked up at the sky again. 'I should get going, but' – he turned to Liam – 'I really enjoyed tonight.'

'Yeah, me too. Maybe next time we can go for a walk instead of just hanging out back here?' suggested Liam.

Julian perked up. 'So you'd like to go out with me again?'

Liam felt his cheeks flush – he was grateful the alley's cool dim lights concealed how red he probably was. 'Yes'

Julian took a step closer and brushed a hand on Liam's face. 'I'd love that.' He leaned forward, his gaze dropping to Liam's mouth, and Liam tilted his head to meet the other man's lips. The kiss was tender, eliciting warm tingles within Liam's body, the likes of which he'd never felt before.

Julian pulled away slowly. 'Goodnight, Liam. See you tomorrow.' Smiling and biting his lip, Julian turned and walked away.

* * *

A few weeks later.

Liam locked up as he and Julian chatted away.

'Victoria is an astute woman, you can't get anything past her,' sighed Julian.

'She was going to find out we were dating at some point,' replied Liam. 'I'm just glad she's all for it and happy for us.'

'She's thirty, right?' Julian folded his arms, leaning against the bricks.

'Thirty-five,' corrected Liam, 'I think.' He scowled, pondering. He shrugged. The two stood leaning their backs against the wall, looking up at the sky. Julian took Liam's hand and interlaced their fingers.

Liam smiled as they stargazed. 'We might not see all the stars here, what with all the city lights, but I'm glad most nights we can see quite a lot.' He angled himself towards Julian. 'We've made this spot ours. It feels nice to stand here with you after work.'

Whether they talked or stood in silence, hanging out back here together brought Liam so much comfort.

Julian beamed at Liam. 'Yesterday was my first day off all week, and all I did was think about you.' Liam smiled as Julian continued. 'I nearly came to the club just so I could be in your presence.'

Liam chuckled. 'It was a busy night, you would have either been bored or Victoria would've roped you into working.'

Julian laughed. 'Wouldn't have been the first time she's done that, rope someone into working just because they were there.'

Julian moved to stand in front of Liam, their hands still interlaced. He placed an arm on the wall and leaned forward. He kissed Liam, who wrapped his other hand around Julian's back.

So far, they had only either hung out here or gone for walks. They would make out, but Julian's kisses would remain light, even the deeper ones. And then Julian had always gone home before dawn.

This time, Julian's kisses became heavy and Liam inhaled sharply, feeling another one of those hot tingles. Julian groaned softly into Liam's mouth, and when he pulled away, his blue eyes almost seemed paler, though they were dark with desire.

'Take me to your place,' Julian demanded in a husky voice.

Liam plunged for Julian's lips and kissed him fiercely. He nearly took him then and there, as the two devoured each other's mouths, kissing hungrily and panting heavily. Taking a few steps forward before stopping to kiss some more, they slowly began down the alley, arms travelling the lengths of their bodies, grasping for bare skin.

They had to run to the apartment if they wanted to have sex indoors, so much had they already started with the foreplay. Once inside, Julian and Liam were tugging each other's clothes off before they had even reached the bedroom. It was their first time being physically intimate together and it was like nothing Liam had ever experienced – it was mind-blowing – and they went at it again and again.

Light glinted on the horizon and they were still at it.

Julian hovered over Liam, smiling tenderly. 'I have never wanted anyone more than I want you.' He lowered himself and kissed Liam, then propped himself up on his elbows again. He looked up at the window, he seemed conflicted.

He stood abruptly, walking over to the window, and lowered the large plastic shades. 'The sunlight, does it engulf the room?'

'Not with that, no,' said Liam. 'Why?'

'I'm not a day person,' Julian replied, 'and after devouring you all night, I just want to lie here and have you in my arms.'

Liam grinned and opened his arms as an invitation. Julian chuckled – god, he looked so sexy standing naked by the window like that, and it took Liam's breath away.

Julian fiddled around with the blinds a bit more. 'Sorry, I like to sleep in dark rooms.'

Liam stood and joined him by the window. 'In that case, do this.' Liam folded the flaps inwards so the plastic would hug the window.

'Perfect,' breathed Julian. The two returned to bed and made love again before finally falling asleep.

* * *

One month later.

Liam and Julian closed up at the club. Julian had finished earlier and waited for Liam so they could stand outside the club in the back alleyway, staring up at the sky like they always did since their very first date, since the night they met.

Liam scrolled through his phone. 'Those mobs are really going at it these days. All the headlines are talking about it. The Cromwell family and the Sharpe family vying for control of several city districts.'

Julian placed his hand over Liam's phone. 'They don't matter right now.' He moved Liam's hand to his pocket where Liam placed his phone. Wrapping his arms around Liam, Julian kissed him. 'Liam,' his expression grew serious, 'I have never felt this way about anyone in my life.'

Liam's stomach fluttered. He smiled. 'I feel the same way, Julian.'

Julian beamed at him and kissed him feverishly. Liam waited to see if Julian said anything more but he didn't. Liam wasn't sure if he should tell him he was in love with him barely a couple of months into their relationship. He was scared to, but at the same time, he was content with how things were for now.

'What if we got our own place?' suggested Julian, breaking his reverie.

Liam smiled. He realised he didn't have to tell him those words right now. If Julian wanted to make future plans with him, then it was because he felt the same way, because he wanted to commit to him.

They had always either stayed here or gone to Liam's. Julian's apartment was far too small – he preferred not to bring Liam back there. Liam had to take his word for it, he had never been. The thought of living together, however, made Liam happier than he'd been in so long.

'If money wasn't a concern, what would you prefer?' asked Julian.

'A house, not an apartment,' said Liam, without needing to think about it.

'Bungalow,' said Julian, 'not a semi-detached.'

'With a backyard and lots of trees.'

'And the bedroom on the west side.'

'We can start saving up,' said Liam, thinking that maybe they would be able to afford it within a year or so.

'We can look to see what's available.' Julian smiled, and they continued to list more requirements for their dream home. In the months that followed, they continued to make plans and browse for houses, dreaming of their future home.

* * *

Several months later.

Liam felt nervous. He and Julian had been to-gether nearly six months now, they had expressed many feelings and had made plans to live together, yet neither had said those words that Liam felt.

His exes had always been too quick to express it, but Liam truly felt it. Even so, he feared it might change things between them. Their relationship was very physical and yet very emotionally charged, even while neither expressed *that* specific emotion in so many words.

'Is something worrying you?' asked Julian. He could always read Liam so well.

He looked so handsome in the glow of the winter night, as slow, light flakes of snow settled on his dark hair, resting for a few seconds before melting away.

'I have something to tell you, Julian. I . . .' Liam hesitated. 'I love you. I'm in love with you.'

Julian beamed at Liam. 'I'm in love with you too.' Liam was so relieved. 'I love you, Liam. I've never loved anyone like this in my life.' He took Liam's face in his hands. 'I love you and I want to live with you.'

Liam's stomach somersaulted with joy. 'I feel the same way.'

Julian's kiss was searing and he and Liam made love right there in the alleyway.

<u>CHAPTER ONE</u>

Present Day.

The silence was both terrifying and soothing at the same time. Liam closed his eyes and leaned against the brick wall as he stood outside the club. It had been busy, with people dancing, shouting, laughing, all drunkenly. Now, the stillness of the winter night dampened whatever sounds came from the boulevard a few streets down.

This was where he had often stood with Julian after their work shifts, talking, laughing, kissing, and making plans for their future together. But Julian was gone, left before dawn a few nights after they had declared their love for each other, left without a word or explanation. Only a scribble on a sticky note saying, *'I have to leave. I'm sorry.'*

It hurt, it still did, even after all these weeks. Julian had never called or answered Liam's calls or texts after that night; Julian had simply disappeared from Liam's life. Liam didn't understand why – he thought they'd been happy.

He had once relished in the quiet after the bustle of work, now he missed hearing Julian's voice or seeing his smile. His heart broke every day again and again. Yet he continued to stand here in the spot they had made theirs.

Liam couldn't help but wonder if things had moved too fast between them – no, he had declared his love six full months after they'd met and started dating. He was just so confused about it all.

Taking a deep breath, he ensured the club was well locked and began down the dark alley. He didn't want to linger too long. There had been murders in the neighbourhood in recent weeks, all gunshot wounds. The rival gangs were at it again. It hadn't stopped the clubgoers, though. Liam figured it was only a matter of time before both mobs decided they wanted to own the club and took their fight to the neighbouring streets.

Liam heard the screech of tires and shouting not too far. He paused, waiting to make sure it was just some drunk folks, but he tensed when he heard a gunshot pierce the stillness.

Looks like the gang fight's here now, he thought to himself.

He quickened his pace and veered the corner into the next alley and came face to face with the man who had left him.

'Julian!' Liam breathed. He swallowed hard, his heart suddenly drumming in his chest.

'Liam.' Julian hesitated. His blue eyes seemed brighter in the darkness of the night and the light in the alley gave his already pale complexion a blue hue, making his handsome features that much more intense, increasing the yearning and anguish in Liam's heart.

Liam was flooded by a wave of emotions. 'What the hell, Julian?' he shouted, tears stinging his eyes.

Julian winced, chagrined, and Liam saw his eyes sparkle with tears.

'Look,' began Julian, taking a step towards Liam, 'I know I owe you an explanation, I just . . . You need to get out of here. I came to get you to safety.'

Liam took a step back, putting two and two together. 'I know what this is,' he seethed. 'You're with the mafias, aren't you?'

'No, I swear, Liam! I'm not with them,' protested Julian. 'I heard about the Cromwells and Sharpes taking their fight here and I came to warn you. Liam, please.' Julian reached for Liam's hand.

Liam pulled away out of reach. 'A little convenient, isn't it?'

Julian grimaced. 'Liam, I promise you—'

'Promise me? I told you I loved you and then you ran!' shouted Liam, his voice hoarse with heartache. His heart felt tight, and it hurt all over again.

Julian merely gaped at him.

'I thought you loved me too,' Liam wept.

'I do. I do *still* love you,' insisted Julian.

'Then why did you leave?' demanded Liam.

'I had . . . priorities.' He caught himself. 'Sorry, that sounds . . . I had . . . a mission.'

'A mission?' Liam repeated, incredulous. 'Crime mission? Or are you with the cops?'

'None of those,' admitted Julian. 'Look, I promise I'll explain everything. Let's just get out of here, go somewhere safe, and I'll explain everything.' He paused and a tear trickled down his cheek – he wiped it away with the back of his thumb. 'I just ask that you trust me.'

'You left, Julian.' The tightness in Liam's chest squeezed harder. 'You claim you love me but you left – why come back now?'

Julian stared at Liam, eyes pleading. 'I had no choice, something . . . took me away for a while, and I realise I should have told you then what it was and why that was, because—'

Gunshot thundering too close for comfort interrupted their tearful exchange.

Julian grabbed Liam's hand and began to run, pulling Liam along with him. 'We have to get out of here. I'm not going to let any harm come to you.'

'Oh, how noble!' spat Liam.

Julian spun on Liam, glaring at him. 'I came back as soon as my mission was complete. I always intended to. I just couldn't tell you then and it's . . . difficult to explain, it would be difficult for you to belie—'

With surprising speed, Julian placed his hand in front of Liam and pushed him against the wall, backing up as a bullet whizzed past them.

Liam stared at Julian, mouth agape. 'Thanks.'

Julian took a beat, looking alarmed, before grabbing hold of Liam's hand again and guiding him out of the alley and bolting onto the street. Shouts coming from nearby told them which way *not* to run as they turned onto the next street over, darting as fast as they could.

Some of the mobsters ran onto the street where they were. Julian skidded to a stop, his eyes darting this way and that, looking hypervigilant. He grabbed Liam's arm and pulled him close, turning around as one of the gang members took aim at them. They ducked behind a parked car.

'We're not with the Sharpes!' Julian shouted. Liam noted how Julian had easily recognised that the ones shooting at them were the Cromwells.

In response, the shooter reloaded his gun.

'Shit!' Julian cursed. He looked towards another parked car. 'If we can get ourselves out of this area,' he told Liam, 'then we—'

The window of the car behind which they hid shattered as another shot resounded behind them.

They ran towards the next car, and then towards another building. Another thunderous roar broke the air as more gang members began shooting at each other. Liam and Julian's assailant continued after them and just as they came up to hide in an alcove, a bullet hit Julian with a thud.

He cried out in pain, bringing his hand to his arm.

'Julian!' Liam cried.

Julian closed his eyes, wincing. 'I'll be fine,' he gritted. He looked over at Liam as they leaned against the wall. 'I'm sorry I never told you the truth. I'm sorry

I left – I'm sorry I hurt you. But I swear I love you and I will tell you *everything*. We just need to get to safety.'

Liam nodded. 'You knew they were coming here. I just can't wrap my head around—'

'I found out just hours ago.' Julian looked at his wound, breathing deeply but looking like the pain wasn't as intense now as it was before. 'I got myself here as quickly as I could.'

'You came to . . . warn me . . .' Liam was just so confused. 'Please, tell me if you're part of a gang of some sort.'

'Of some sort,' Julian repeated pensively. 'Not a mafia, no. Not a . . . It's complicated.' Julian pinched his fingers and reached into his wound and pulled out the bullet with nothing more than a small groan. 'I'm good.'

Suddenly, the barrel of a handgun emerged from the corner – the shooter was pointing it straight at Julian's head, his grip on the handgun firm and steady.

Liam froze.

Julian stared the other man in the eyes. 'Big mistake,' he sneered.

With exceptional speed, he grabbed the assailant's arm, pulling and twisting. The Cromwell crony cried out, dropping the gun, and Julian grabbed his neck and twisted hard. The man fell dead on the ground before him.

Liam stared at Julian. 'And you say you're not a cop or with a mob,' he said, unconvinced. He pointed at the dead shooter, his eyes never leaving Julian's. 'Explain that!'

'Not here.'

Julian picked up the dead man's gun and began to run; Liam followed close behind. A car turned onto the street and mobsters began to shoot at anyone who was nearby.

'Fuck!' Julian shouted. Shielding Liam as they continued to run, Julian took aim and began shooting at the mobsters within the vehicle, hitting his mark every time.

'Now I know there's definitely something you're not telling me,' Liam muttered as they ran.

'There is, and I promise I'll tell you,' replied Julian. He secured the clip and aimed afresh, again not missing his target.

Liam's throat and lungs were burning but he pushed forward. They turned another corner as the car behind them crashed into a fence.

Liam stopped before Julian, facing him. 'The truth now, Julian!'

Panting, Julian stared at Liam. 'We need to get away from here,' he insisted.

'I'm not moving until you tell me what's going on.'

Fear flashed in Julian's eyes. 'You're not going to believe me without the full explanation.'

'Then quit stalling and explain already!' demanded Liam.

Julian worked his jaw. 'I'm—'

A deafening gunshot exploded – Liam felt a sharp, burning sensation in his gut, and his knees buckled beneath him as he struggled to stay upright.

'No!' screamed Julian.

He caught Liam before he could hit the ground, gently setting him down. Liam's breath came out syncopated as he realised what had just happened. He screamed in pain – a loud guttural scream – then winced, clenching his jaw.

'No, no, this is what I was trying to prevent,' Julian quavered, opening up Liam's jacket and staring at the wound. 'I can't lose you.'

'Lose me? You left me.'

Julian let out a tearful breath. 'I left on a mission I couldn't tell you about. I'm so sorry, Liam.'

Liam glanced down at his stomach as his blood rapidly drenched his clothes. Seeing it only made his heart pump harder and the blood gush faster, and Liam's breath came out shakily.

Julian pulled Liam close to his chest, picking him up off the ground, and began to run. Liam didn't know if it was the dizziness of blood loss that altered his perceptions but he felt like they were moving a lot faster than was normal. He saw houses whizz by his vision and then trees as they entered the forest. The sounds of guns and shouting mobsters grew distant until, finally, the quiet of the night was all that remained.

Julian placed Liam down on the snow, which quickly turned red from his blood. Julian's jaw was clenched.

The pain Liam felt was immeasurable, yet somehow he couldn't bring himself to scream again, and he was so sweat-soaked from fear, he barely noticed the cold.

'I should never have waited this long to tell you the truth, Liam.' Julian looked down at Liam's wound, his tears dripping onto it.

Liam tried to speak but a mere whimper escaped him as tears stung his eyes.

Julian's voice came out determined yet half-whispered. 'I'm not going to let you die.'

'I think,' Liam winced, his voice laboured, 'it's too late for that.'

'No!' Something flashed in Julian's eyes. Liam lifted a bloodied hand to Julian's face; Julian placed his hand on his. 'I came back because I love you . . . because I owe you the truth. So here is the truth.'

His eyes flashed again and paled, brightening, his pupils becoming as blue as his irises and nearly as pale. He let his mouth hang open, and smoothly his top canines extended. Liam's eyes widened and he gaped at Julian.

'You're a—' he gasped.

'Yes. I can save your life, but tell me no and I won't, as much as that grieves me. I won't force this life on you.'

Liam gritted his teeth as a wave of pain threatened to pull him into unconsciousness. 'Do it!'

Julian leaned down towards him and gently placed his teeth on his skin. He paused. Liam felt Julian's breath on his neck before an intense sting.

He winced, grabbing Julian's arm tightly. He felt Julian's lips wrap around the punctures and the pain eased. As Julian sucked his blood, Liam relaxed in his caress.

Julian kissed Liam's neck tenderly before pulling away. 'It's done,' he said softly.

Liam waited, his body trembling lightly. Then he began to shake, but not from pain, from some sort of power that coursed through his veins. It was a vibration that came from inside of him that he felt gushing through all his veins. In his mouth, Liam felt his eyeteeth extend, and there was a mild prickle in his eyes that he just knew was the same kind of flare he'd seen in Julian's eyes.

Liam looked down at his wound, feeling an uncomfortable sensation. The bullet appeared at the opening of the hole in his stomach and fell out. Then the wound closed and Liam felt himself heal inside his body. It wasn't pleasant but the discomfort quickly passed.

Liam swallowed hard, breathing in deeply. He stared at Julian.

He wasn't sure which of them sprung towards the other first but their lips met and their mouths opened to let the other in, and they kissed fervently. The familiar tingling in Liam's stomach told him how much he loved and wanted Julian.

He pulled away. Julian leaned his forehead on his.

'I am so sorry, Liam, that I never told you the truth.'

'You should have trusted that I'd believe you,' Liam placed his hand on Julian's face, 'that I'd still love you despite who or what you are.' Liam grimaced at the blood he'd smeared on Julian who didn't seem to mind.

Julian kissed Liam again. 'I love you, Liam. I promise I'll never leave your side again.'

Liam let that sink in, realising the implications of this new situation. 'I guess that means we're geared to spend eternity together.'

Julian's lips quirked into a side grin. 'Is that a proposal?'

Liam chuckled, feeling flutters all over his body. 'It is if you want it to be.'

Julian beamed at him, and with his heightened senses Liam could feel the truth and their love reverberate and pulse between them.

Liam pressed a long and ardent kiss to Julian's lips, wrapping his arms around him, deepening the kiss with each passing moment, and his tongue traced his lover's vampiric canines as they hungrily devoured each other's mouths.

Liam drew back and met Julian's gaze. 'You owe me one hell of an explanation.'

Julian let out a small laugh. 'That, I do.'

Julian helped Liam to his feet and he beckoned him to follow. He held out his hand and Liam took it, interlacing their fingers. They walked through the snow in the forest, the silence of the night no longer terrifying Liam, and Julian's voice soothingly cut through the stillness as he began his story.

CHAPTER TWO

Julian and Liam stood before Wilbur in the coven's manor common room as the vampire elder studied Liam from down his nose, his gaze scrutinising.

Always handsomely dressed in a cardigan, Wilbur was a gentleman with a sophisticated accent that had earned him the respect of the many. His grey matted hair fell neatly by his ears, though he kept the top of his hair slicked back. His round glasses gave him the look of the title he had earned a degree in and taught for many years – he was a history professor, specifically teaching mediaeval times. As a vampire elder, he knew many hidden arts and knowledge few vampires became worthy of learning or eligible to receive.

'And you say he consented before you turned him?' Wilbur asked Julian, his eyes always on Liam.

'Yes,' replied Julian, keeping his assertive stance, yet feeling a bit nervous all the same. Wilbur was his mentor, a former teacher, and the vampire who turned him. He had as much respect as he did admiration for the man and the authority he represented among the vampire elders.

Wilbur nodded. 'Very well.' He held out his hand to Liam. 'Welcome to the coven, Liam.'

Liam shook his hand. 'Thank you, sir.'

'Oh,' scoffed Wilbur, 'just Wilbur will do.' He chuckled. 'Don't look so worried, I don't bite – well, not other vampires, that is.' He guffawed. 'You explained to him how things work, yes?'

'Regarding the sun thing?' asked Liam.

Julian had explained the basics to Liam – the rules of the coven, the sources of blood that could feed a vampire, what powers Liam might develop, which legends were accurate and which were not, such as their tears being actual tears and not blood, as well as how silver poisons them and what happens to them when exposed to the sun.

Wilbur smiled at Liam. 'It's much better than what the stories say, don't you think? Those stories are there to give the impression that any vampire would die instantly in the sun, it gives a semblance of safe feeling to mortals.'

Vampires had a few hours before succumbing to the sun, in fact – its effects were far more sinister than Julian had ever imagined before being turned.

First, the vampire's skin would burn, then blister, then their insides would boil. It was a much longer process and a lot more painful if you couldn't find cover to get out of the sun. A vampire usually weakened first and then died within a couple of hours.

Only human blood could give them the necessary strength to heal enough to survive – at best. Julian had seen a fellow vampire convulse, and then vomit vital organs, as her skin had turned into one massive pus-oozing boil.

Wilbur inclined his head forward. 'A skin disease or U.V. sensitivity is much more plausible as a justification if we must scurry to the safety of the shadows, thus making any vampire appear as any other mortal – hiding in plain sight, as it were. If ever we do need to step out at a most critical and dangerous time . . .' He opened his hands, as though presenting the explanation he'd just given.

Julian had personally never taken the risk, though the coven elders had been forced to brave the sun on a few occasions – they had returned looking like Undead and barely alive, but they were alive.

'But anyway,' Wilbur carried on cheerily, 'has Julian filled you in on all the latest?'

'As far as I can tell,' Liam replied carefully.

Julian opened his mouth to interject but Wilbur was quick to reply.

'Excellent! I mean, it *does* involve the club you work at.' Wilbur turned back to Julian. 'Julian—'

'Actually,' began Julian.

'—What's the status on the two mafias in the New Collective district?'

Julian winced internally as Liam gave him an angry stare.

They had travelled for a couple of nights, stopping at safehouses before reaching the coven's manor.

Julian had *mostly* filled Liam in, but he had wanted to report back to Wilbur before letting Liam in on the finer details regarding his mission. He knew it would be a lot for Liam to take in, being a newly turned vampire, and Julian had not wanted to overwhelm him with everything at once.

Julian gave Liam an apologetic smile but his lover's gaze remained one of indignation.

'I knew you had something to do with those criminals,' he hissed.

'It's not like that, Liam,' insisted Julian. 'I swear. We are not part of those mobs. It's just . . . the safehouse of the district . . . I was stationed there, that's how we met.'

'Right.'

'I was to work at a key location where it would be easy to have an ear on the ground and hide my identity as a vampire while still monitoring the two crime groups.'

'And you made that place Nightly Glow Club.'

'It allowed me to meet *you*,' Julian tried but Liam's expression never changed. 'The Sharpes and Cromwells going for the club is a coincidence.' Julian paused, agonised. He could hear Liam's heartbeat increase as his anger rose. 'Those gangs are onto us, they suspect something and they're drawing unwanted attention to our coven.'

Liam merely crossed his arms.

'They've begun rumours of supernatural beings,' Wilbur explained, his voice diplomatic, 'throwing out names like werewolves, undead, vampires, fae folk, you name it. If we don't quell this soon, we risk being discovered, or worse, exposed.'

'Is that such a bad thing, though?' demanded Liam, his green eyes flaring momentarily.

Wilbur sighed. 'You'll learn quickly that our kin are not trusted by mortals and those who become aware of our existence would rather we be exterminated.'

Liam scowled. Wilbur placed a hand on his shoulder, continuing. 'Like any group, there are some vampires who don't respect consent, who would rather murder, and drink human blood rather than feed on animal blood or find willing participants who gladly donate their blood to us or let us drink directly from them. There are those who paint the name vampire as monsters, and mortals fear us.'

The elder vampire withdrew but kept his eyes on Liam. 'We cannot risk them finding out, especially bloodthirsty mobsters who want an excuse to murder others in cold blood.'

'That's a lot of blood analogies for a vampire,' seethed Liam.

Wilbur looked from Liam to Julian, his gaze sympathetic. 'I'll let you two sort this out before we meet with the rest of the coven. Again, welcome, Liam. I'm sorry for the adjustments you'll have to make to your lifestyle, but we're here to support you in your new journey as one of us.'

He left the room. Liam hissed, passing a hand through his blond hair as he started towards the exit at the far side of the room.

'You're mad,' concluded Julian, feeling a pang of worry.

Liam spun around, continuing to walk backwards. 'I don't know, Julian, maybe.' His tone was resentful. 'You lied to me.'

'What was I supposed to say, Liam, huh?' Julian spread his arms out, feeling exasperated. "Hey Liam, I'm in love with you – by the way, I'm a vampire. Oh, and mobsters are threatening to expose us to the public." Doesn't exactly follow well after a declaration of love, does it?'

'You had countless opportunities to tell me, but no, you chose to leave me.'

'You're still angry about that,' Julian ascertained. 'Again, I didn't leave *you*, I just . . . left.'

'And then you tell me . . . *after* I get shot at and am on the verge of death!' Liam stopped walking. 'And then you still omit details that form a full truth.'

'I made a mistake, Liam, I realise that now.' Julian felt his lower lip tremble. 'Please, forgive me.'

Liam gave no reply but turned back around and walked towards the door. Julian's heart sank as he followed; he understood it was going to take a bit more time before Liam forgave him for everything.

Liam stopped at the door, putting his hand out to stop Julian. 'I'd like to be on my own right now, Julian.' Julian felt another pang. Liam didn't wait for his reply, he simply left the room. Julian hung his head low.

For the few nights they had travelled, Liam had seemed . . . amenable to the changes he was experiencing, and Julian was helping him adapt and adjust. Julian realised that now that the adrenaline had left, and that Liam learnt the details Julian had omitted to tell him, understandably, he was angry again.

'I take it he's still upset?' inquired Wilbur, returning to the common room.

'I thought you had a meeting led by the elders to prepare for,' retorted Julian.

Wilbur held up his hands in defence. 'I'm not the eldest of the elders. I'm barely even grey.'

'Very funny,' muttered Julian, a hint of derision in his voice.

Wilbur clapped Julian on the back. 'He'll come around. It's a lot to process, being turned. Remember when I turned you?'

'That was different, though,' said Julian, 'you weren't the man I fell in love with.'

'No, maybe,' began Wilbur, sitting on the edge of the desk that stood near the fireplace, 'but I was your teacher and mentor.'

'Yeah, I did wonder for the longest time why you only gave classes at night.'

Wilbur chuckled. 'It was the hippy thing to do, I suppose.' He shook his head. 'A very different time than when *I* was turned. The centuries were not kind back then. You're lucky you knew better times.' Wilbur spread out his arms in a half-shrug. 'We adapt, we change as life around us changes. Liam has just been thrown into this world. And he didn't have months to think about it like you did. It was that or death.'

The knot in Julian's stomach twisted even further. 'You don't think he regrets it, do you?'

Wilbur sighed, stepping forward and placing his hand on Julian's shoulder. 'I think he's in shock and needs to take it all in.'

'What are you two conspiring about now?' demanded Stella with a chuckle as she entered the common room. The tall white-haired woman crossed her arms. 'Was that him I saw out in the corridor? The new lad, Julian's concubine?'

Julian rolled his eyes. 'Oh, for real, Stella, get with the times.'

'Honestly, it would do society a great deal of good to adopt some of my century's expressions,' retorted Stella.

'Says the woman who walks around with a snuff box,' replied Wilbur

'It was fashionable back in my day,' protested Stella. 'Anyone who was anyone walked around parading their fancy snuff boxes.'

'It'll get you arrested today,' reminded Julian.

Stella waved a dismissive hand. She was a beautiful woman in her mid-life before she was turned. She had been rich, had had prestige, and had found herself attacked by vampires who had been careless – she turned as a matter of course and then retaliated. Thus, she had gained a reputation among the elders of the coven.

'Anyway, I believe I saw him go out in the gardens with Chad.'

'What?' snapped Julian. 'Not Chad!'

'Oh, give over, he's harmless,' chided Stella.

'Harmless! He flirts with everything that moves!'

'True. He is after all the best-looking vampire in the coven, and always manages to get in anyone's pants – anyone he fancies.'

'Not helping, Stella,' Wilbur warned under his breath.

Stella gesticulated animatedly, not even taking a breath between her thoughts. 'I mean, who can blame them, he's got that curly hair Adonis look going with a taupe complexion because he's more ancient than Ancient Greece itself. It certainly got *me* tangled up in the sheets with him.'

'I'm going after them!' Julian started off.

'Don't forget the meeting,' Wilbur reminded.

'I don't care about that right now!'

Julian dashed to the garden, stopping at a copse of trees by some hedges near the fountain. The estate had large and elaborate grounds, perfect for training new vampires like Liam.

It was the coven's main base; a lavish manor Stella had insisted they use – she would only demand the best. She was among the top elders; Wilbur was among the lesser elders. Some of the oldest vampires in the coven were more than a millennium old, though the coven elders always elected two or three vampires to pose as the leaders. Stella, Wilbur, and another elder named Richard were among those leaders.

Chad was also an elder, turned at age forty, though he could easily pass for mid-thirties, and as a vampire, his age was anyone's guess. He had a flirtatious reputation and had taken on many lovers during his existence.

Julian spotted them. The elder vampire had curly hair as dark as his grey eyes that shone beneath thick eyebrows, sleek and flawless skin that always seemed to glisten, with a mild taupe tone with violet undertones that always made him look like a deity. He wore a loosely buttoned mother-of-pearl shirt as he often did that stuck out from under an as loosely zipped thick black jacket, leaving his collar exposed despite the cold weather, with flexible dark grey pants that could pass as tight slacks from afar.

Chad wore a charming lopsided grin as he gazed into Liam's eyes, a hand on his shoulder and the other on his chest. He leaned forward to speak in a conspiratorial tone.

Julian shook his head, seething. He would not let Chad steal his man.

Julian dashed with vampiric speed and pulled the other vampire off Liam, throwing him to the ground.

'Hands off my boyfriend, Chad!' Julian bared his canines at Chad, growling as though he were a werewolf and letting his eyes flare with a vampiric glow.

'Relax, I only go after the single ones.' Chad stood, dusting the dirt off his clothes. 'Hasn't our friendship taught you that by now?' Chad feigned dejection, placing a hand on his heart. 'I'm wounded.'

Ignoring Chad, Julian faced Liam who looked aghast.

'What the hell, Julian!' Liam shouted.

'Liam, please, let's talk.'

'I don't want to talk right now, and . . .' His face contorted in disdain. 'I am *not* your boyfriend.'

'What?' breathed Julian, shock and dismay hitting him like a punch in the gut.

'I'm your *fiancé!*' shouted Liam. Julian blinked, letting that sink in. 'Or did you forget that we pledged each other to each other for eternity back there?' Liam pointed behind him towards the general distance from a few days ago. 'Unless I imagined all that and I'm the only one to have interpreted it that way?'

'No, you're right. I'm sorry.' Julian remembered very well promising Liam he'd never leave his side and Liam saying they'd spend eternity together. Julian was the one to suggest it was a proposal. *It is if you want it to be,* Liam had said, confirming his intention to truly spend eternity with Julian.

'Just go, Julian. I need time to let this all sink in, okay.'

Julian blinked back tears and nodded. 'Okay,' he whispered.

Julian returned to the manor, shaking with unrest. He leaned his head against the wall and pinched the bridge of his nose, letting a few tears run down his cheeks. He stood there, outside, trying to quell his fear for what felt like the whole night, yet the moon was still high in the sky when Liam and Chad returned.

Julian pushed away from the wall – he hadn't meant to make it look like he'd been waiting for him.

'Can we talk?' Liam asked gently.

'Yeah.'

Chad took his cue, nodding to both of them before going in a separate direction.

Julian and Liam re-entered the manor and walked a few paces before Liam turned to face him.

'Look, just because I'm angry at you doesn't mean I regret any of it. I just need time to adjust.' He stole a brief glance behind his shoulder and promptly returned his gaze forward. 'I don't know what your history with Chad is, but he didn't flirt – if you're jealous about him showing me around.'

'Look, I'm sorry I over-reacted,' admitted Julian.

'Julian, I love you, that hasn't changed,' asserted Liam.

'I know, I just . . .'

'And then you called me your *boyfriend,*' said Liam, 'and that hurt me . . . because I thought . . .' He trailed off, looking away, his long bangs hiding his eyes.

'I guess we never made it official. I was worried that . . .' began Julian, his heart drumming in his chest. 'You *are* my fiancé.'

'Then let's *make* it official,' demanded Liam. He took Julian's hands in his.

'Okay.' Julian agreed. He took a breath to ask the question properly this time.

'Will you marry me, Julian?' Liam said before Julian could ask him.

Julian smiled but his eyes blurred with tears all the same. 'Yes.'

Liam kissed Julian, and the older vampire felt the fire of their love vibrate throughout his entire body. This moment was perfect; Julian had voiced wanting a proposal, and Liam had provided it, and Julian could truly feel his lover's love and true intent and desire behind his words, even more now as they kissed.

'Aw, I'm glad you two made up,' said Wilbur, passing by. 'Remember, meeting in thirty minutes. Don't be late – our newest member cannot miss his first coven meeting, after all. Ta-ra.' And he continued on his jovial way.

Thinking quickly, feeling the intensity of his desire, Julian grabbed Liam by the arm and pulled him into an adjacent study, slamming the door behind them. He pressed Liam against the wall and devoured his mouth.

'Julian,' breathed Liam. 'Don't we have that meeting?'

'He said thirty minutes, and I intend to celebrate with my fiancé.' Julian plunged back towards Liam's mouth. Liam gasped, pulling away for air. Julian grinned. 'I'm your vampire fiancé and I'm in a sucking mood.'

Liam chuckled. 'Do you realise how corny that sounds?'

'What can I say, I grew up during a time when being corny was a turn-on.'

'Then suck!' demanded Liam, tugging on Julian's belt, sending searing tingles pulsing in his pelvis.

Both men chuckled gruffly as they eagerly tore each other's clothes off.

Julian paused only to quickly double-check that the door was locked before pressing Liam back against the wall and rubbing their naked bodies together.

'Oh, Julian,' moaned Liam. 'It's been ages since I felt your body like that against mine.'

Julian paused, biting his lower lip. 'We did kind of hurry here, didn't we?'

'The trip was exhausting, what with learning to be a vampire and all. Holding you in my arms was all I could manage.' Liam kissed Julian's neck.

Julian nibbled Liam's earlobe. 'So how does it feel to properly make up after all that time apart?'

'Oh god, Julian, even just touching you is making me tremble.'

Julian chuckled. 'That's what being a vampire does to you.'

He grabbed Liam's hands and pinned them above his head, kissing him the whole time. Both vampires moaned into each other's mouths.

Lowering himself, Julian grabbed Liam's skin with his teeth near his collarbone, then at his pecs, then his stomach. His lover's perfectly shaved erection pulsed as though begging him to take him. Grabbing hold of Liam's ass, Julian enveloped his lips around Liam's length. Liam groaned and Julian looked up to see him tilt his head back as he sucked him.

'Oh, fuck, Julian.' Liam hit the wall with his hand. 'Oh my god, nnh!' His green eyes flared and paled, and his canines extended.

Julian pulled out for a quick moment to revel at his fiancé's body. 'Fuck, you're sexy!' Julian opened his mouth to swallow Liam's cock again.

Liam began to pant louder, his hips moving as Julian sucked him vigorously. Julian would have liked to take his time with him, but they were in a bit of a hurry.

Julian extended his canines and let the smooth sides glide along Liam's cock as he sucked him – his lover's length fit perfectly between them. The moans escaping Liam's mouth and the way he was sliding himself up and down the wall, frantically jerking his head and clawing at the wall, told Julian he enjoyed it. It urged him to continue.

Julian sucked faster, grabbing hold of Liam's length with one hand and his own with the other. He moaned onto Liam's cock and the man stiffened in his mouth. Julian's mouth filled with the warm fluid of his fiancé's elation and Liam stifled a shout.

Before Julian had swallowed, Liam bent with vampiric speed and grabbed Julian's erection.

'*I* will finish you.' The look in his eyes was so arousing, Julian nearly spilled right then.

Liam took Julian's erection in his mouth, letting his saliva drip onto every part of his length. Then he slowly pulled him out.

Tugging gently upwards, Liam led Julian to rise before turning around. 'Take me,' he commanded, placing his hands on the wall and presenting his ass to Julian.

Julian was already seeping and he knew he didn't need much more to reach his climax. Eyes on Liam, Julian bent to reach into his pant pocket and pulled out the small tube of lubricant he had with him.

'You have a tube of lube on you?' Liam gaped at him from over his shoulder.

'Uh, yeah.' Julian rose from his crouch. 'I *was* hoping for make up sex once I'd explained everything to you.' He bit his lower lip in nervousness. 'I wanted to plan for any scenario. I know we don't always need it but we *are* going a bit fast today.'

The look in Liam's eyes was voracious. 'Fuck, Julian. Just lather yourself up and take me.'

Julian exhaled a syncopated breath as his cock pulsed in anticipation, seeping another drip of precum. Julian pulled the cap off the tube and squeezed for just enough. He spread the lube over his oozing cock, nearly making himself come in the process as his hand lathered the slippery substance. Then, casting the tube of lube aside, he aligned himself with Liam's inviting hole.

Julian slowly slid his length into Liam's rectum; both men groaned loudly. Julian thrust once, pulled halfway out, and thrust again. Heat rose through his body. He thrust again as his pelvis throbbed in elation. He pulled out a bit and thrust once more.

Burying his face in the nape of Liam's neck and gripping his shoulders from underneath his arms, Julian erupted into his lover's anus, screaming into his neck. He let his pelvis pulse on its own as he whimpered the rest of his orgasm before pulling himself out.

Liam turned around, leaning his back against the wall and breathing heavily. He pulled Julian to him, his lips crashing against his as both let out another muffled howl into each other's mouths.

Dripping with sweat, Julian held Liam's naked body flush against his.

'I love you, Liam,' he panted.

'I love you, Julian,' replied Liam, equally out of breath.

Julian quickly checked his watch. 'Five minutes.'

'I guess we'll continue later,' suggested Liam.

Julian grinned at him and chuckled. He nibbled his lover's lower lip. 'I love you so much, my fiancé.'

Liam bit his lip, looking more attractive and enticing than ever before, with his newly formed canines extended out and his long sun blond side bangs hanging low enough to meet them – Julian wanted to make love to him again right now, ready for more. But the meeting . . .

Julian and Liam quickly yet reluctantly dressed after wiping themselves off with some tissues from the box that stood on the study's desk. They used spit to help clean themselves – it would have to do until they retired to their private room after the meeting where they would be able to bathe . . . and make love once more.

With haste, they headed out for the meeting, giddy and barely able to contain their desire, teasing each other with looks and holding each other's hands tightly. It was going to be one hell of a long meeting, no matter how short it lasted.

CHAPTER THREE

It had been a few days now since Liam and Julian had arrived at the coven's manor; Liam was already adapting and feeling at home among his new fellow vampires. Julian sat next to Liam, fingers interlaced with his, as they waited for the elders in charge to arrive.

This meeting was taking place in a different room than the one from the other day, with only a few attendees present. All the chairs were arranged in a circular formation. Chad sat to Julian's right, and a young woman with burgundy auburn hair eating a lollipop sat to Liam's left – she looked no older than twenty years of age. Then there were, whom he was told were, twins – a man and woman perhaps in their mid-thirties in terms of appearance. Finally, sat a mid-forties man dressed in an impeccable business suit. This final vampire was Richard, the coven's third leading elder.

Stella entered the conference room.

'Stella, looking beautiful as always,' remarked Chad as he acknowledged her.

'You're just saying that because we once had a thing.' She smiled though it did not reach her eyes.

'You've dated Stella?' asked Liam.

'Well don't look so surprised,' retorted Chad.

'He's dated half the coven,' the female twin said, suppressing a laugh. She and her brother shared a knowing look and giggled, leaning conspiratorially towards each other to whisper something Liam didn't hear. The scene amused him.

'You like all of them older or just the women?' Liam inquired, leaning towards Chad and keeping his voice low.

'Any age, really – twenties, thirties, all the way to seventies. I've had men, women, those who fall anywhere in between or anyone out of that, you name it – I enjoy them all.'

'You're ancient, right?' asked Liam. 'Chad doesn't sound very ancient.'

'It's derived from Cad,' replied Chad, 'which has had altered derivatives and pronunciations over the millennia. I like Chad. Few have ever known me as Cad.' Liam pursed his lips, nodding.

Wilbur entered the room and he and Stella faced the semi-circle, remaining on their feet. Richard stood and joined them, standing beside Wilbur. Stella cleared her throat, giving Chad a pointed stare, her white hair shining brightly under the ceiling light. Everyone fell silent.

'We have news of the mobsters' operations,' Stella announced, 'and a plan.' Her eyes landed on Julian. 'But you're not going to like it.'

Next to Liam, Julian stirred. 'Why wouldn't I like it?' he asked in suspicion.

'Because it involves Nightly Glow Club where you two worked,' replied Wilbur. Julian's grip on Liam's hand tightened. 'They've taken over it.'

'Which gang,' demanded Julian. 'Last I checked both the Cromwells *and* the Sharpes were vying for it.'

'The Sharpes have taken it,' stated Richard, his accent aristocratic. 'The shootout resulted in the Sharpes winning – they have secured control and allies in the entirety of the New Collective District. We know but little of what the Cromwells know about us, and we know even less of what the Sharpes know about us.'

'The Sharpes are a large family with many allies who already owned many businesses around the city,' explained Wilbur. 'Their operations thus far seem more legal and less lethal than those of the Cromwells, but it doesn't mean they aren't a threat to vampires.'

'They are a secretive group and have acted strategically over the years,' Richard went on. 'It is only wise for us to get close where it makes sense for us to do so, and learn whatever we can about their plans and their syndicate.'

'I will act as a patron and begin visiting regularly.' Stella shifted her focus to Liam. 'While you may have been M.I.A. for close to a week now, you haven't been removed from the roster.'

Julian drew in a sharp breath. 'No, no. Oh no. You are *not* sending Liam in the thick of things!'

'Liam can pose as an employee and continue his shifts there,' explained Stella, 'and find out information from the inside. They don't know his face as one of us. They know all of yours.'

'How do you know I haven't been fired?' inquired Liam, curious as to how the elders got their information.

'I called to ask to speak with you,' said Stella, 'and they told me you had been absent and weren't returning their calls. Your manager asked if I was a relative because she was concerned about you. I told her I was a friend of yours.'

'That's Victoria for you, more worried about our well-being than being short-staffed,' muttered Liam.

'Okay, so sending Liam in makes sense,' voiced Chad, 'but aren't your tastes a bit fancy for a club like that? No offence, but you're more of a speakeasy type of gal.'

Stella flashed him a flirtatious grin. 'Being permanently fifty years old has its perks, Chad.'

'There are perks to being permanently forty,' Chad teased back.

'I *was* a burlesque dancer once,' Stella reminded him.

Chad blushed, his grin wide. 'I remember.'

The young woman beside Liam sighed as though half-snoring. 'Stop flirting already,' she muttered under her breath.

Stella continued, ignoring the comment. 'You just watch me put my skills to good use; I'll be undercover, and keeping an eye on Liam.'

Julian hissed. 'You are not sending Liam undercover in there', he objected. 'He hasn't had proper training. He won't be able to control his senses when he smells trouble or feels fear; even *I* have trouble sometimes.' His eyes flashed more pale.

'He's a fast learner, this one,' noted Chad, 'if you're worried about him handling himself.'

'Julian,' said Liam, his voice calm yet assertive, 'I want to know what this entails and I want to be the one to decide.'

Julian turned his head to Liam, his grip on his hand even tighter. 'Liam, I almost lost you the other night. I can't . . .' He shook his head.

Liam placed his free hand on Julian's cheek and soothed him by rubbing his thumb gently. 'I'm sure they'll train me a bit before I get back to work. Stella will be a regular – she'll have my back.'

'And the rest of us will be close by,' said the girl sitting next to Liam. She winked. 'I'm Mandy, by the way.'

'Nice to meet you.'

'Likewise!' She grinned at him, her eyes darting up and down as she sucked on her lollipop.

'Hey, no flirting, Mandy,' Chad playfully chided, 'or you'll get the same earful I got from Julian.' His eyes bulged for a second and he let out a *tsk*.

'Whatevs,' said Mandy, shrugging. She giggled.

Wilbur deliberately cleared his throat, drawing everyone's attention back.

'Security footage shows Julian's face shooting at a car full of Cromwell members,' Wilbur explained, 'but Liam is obscured. As their rivals, the Sharpes are glad they got eliminated. Both crime syndicates, while they are at war, have different proof of our existence. Like Richard explained, we know little of what they know beyond having proof, but we *do* know this: the Cromwells want to expose the vampires. Who knows what the Sharpes want to do with that information.'

Wilbur cast his eyes on the twins. 'Zack, Zanitha, you two need to get in with the rival mob, the Cromwells; they know your faces but not as vampires.'

'We'll get in, get close, and find out everything we can about what they know,' asserted Zack.

'Liam,' said Stella, 'what's your story if you go back to work?'

'Well, this time last year I got hit with a massive stomach bug, which lasted days. And you say they think I'm unwell again, so I'll spin a similar tale.'

'Good. Come with me, I'll teach you the basics of keeping your instincts in check, meaning keeping your eyes human-looking and your canines retracted.'

'What? Now?!' exclaimed Julian.

'Julian, I'll be fine,' Liam reassured him, rubbing his thumb on his knuckles.

Julian stood abruptly, letting go of Liam's hand, and glared at the coven leaders, pointing an accusatory finger at them. 'If my fiancé dies because of your plan, *I* will be the one to expose the vampires and have all the authorities storm the manor.'

Wilbur, Richard and Stella looked nonplussed. Stella sighed. She waved her hand dismissively. 'The last time you threatened us, it was because we put young Davita in the spotlight.'

'She's just a little girl!' insisted Julian.

'Who happens to be over a thousand years old,' Wilbur reminded him. 'Look, we understand your concern—'

'Concern! Concern?' seethed Julian. 'This is not "concern".' His eyes flared and he balled his hands into fists. 'This is fear for the life of the man I love.' His canines extended. 'And I will protect him with my life! I will take all the silver bullets for him, I will—'

'Julian!' shouted Liam. Julian stopped and turned back to Liam, his paled eyes filled with torment. Liam stood and took Julian's face in his hands. 'I want to do this. I can help my new coven. Let me do this. I promise if things get sticky, I'll get out of there before anyone knows I'm a vampire.'

'You saw what they're capable of, Liam,' Julian mewled. 'You could have died!'

'But I didn't, because you saved me and gave me new life.'

Julian closed his eyes. 'I hate this,' he whispered.

'Then you are agreed,' concluded Wilbur. 'Let's begin.'

Julian let out a guttural sigh, reluctantly letting go of Liam's hands. Liam gave him a kiss on the cheek and then left with Stella.

* * *

The first thing Liam did was call work. He lamented his stomach to Victoria – at least she was still his boss, despite the Sharpes taking over the club – and said he was feeling much better now.

'Happens every year,' she confirmed. 'I figured it was that. But next time, call. There have been . . . some changes around here. I'll explain when you get here. Can you start again tomorrow?'

The club was always only open at night, and Liam had the nightfall shift, meaning 10:00 p.m. to whatever time Victoria decided. Going back to work without the need to ask for shift changes was the easy part.

Liam had some quick training with the other vampires: fighting, dodging, using his vampiric speed, which he had not practised before – at least he could move more quickly now. Controlling his instincts while remaining alert was the main lesson.

When he and Julian had travelled to the manor, they had taken their time, and taken detours since cops and mobsters would be searching for them – Julian couldn't take any public transportation or routes where the mobs controlled the sectors.

Thankfully for Liam, he could return into town in a warm bus, and it only took a few hours to return to his apartment. He already missed Julian. His heart felt heavy at knowing they would not see much of each other for several days at a time if not longer, though something told him he might not see him for at least another few weeks, given the circumstances.

Since the mobsters knew Julian's face as a vampire, Liam had to maintain the semblance that Julian had left him, not to mention pretending he had not seen or spoken to him since.

Liam remembered Julian's anger as he was leaving. Julian had clenched his fists, seething at the elders. 'I hate this. I hate that you're sending him.' And he had threatened them again. Apparently, Julian's threats were a usual occurrence regarding those for whom he cared. It brought comfort to Liam to think about it.

Liam smiled thinking of his fiancé as he walked into the club through the back entrance.

'Welcome back,' Victoria said to him, her long blonde hair so perfectly coiffed as always. 'How's your tummy?'

Liam placed his hand on his stomach, on the place where he had been shot. 'A lot better, thanks.'

'Good. We have a new manager – he's going to be taking shifts with me – and a new associate,' explained Victoria.

She led him to a table where sat a handsomely rugged man with medium-length brown hair and an impressive woman whose dark hair was long enough to rival Lady Godiva's. The man's tawny complexion mirrored the older woman's, who seemed to be in her late-forties, while the man looked to be in his thirties, though it was hard to tell. One thing was certain, he was built and looked very strong.

The man reclined in the booth, his elbows propped up on the backrest. His sleeves were half rolled up, exposing his arm hair and an expensive-looking watch. His mannerisms were much more laid-back than those of the woman at his side who sat with perfect posture. Liam also clocked the black-matte handguns holstered at their hips, tucked in leather waistbands.

'This is Liam Donahue,' Victoria presented, 'the one I was telling you about.'

'The one with the tummy bug,' said the woman, standing and reaching her hand out to clasp Liam's. 'I'm Adrienne Sharpe, nice to meet you. I'm the new associate.'

Liam tensed at the mention of the name, even if he knew to expect it. The Sharpes were vicious when they wanted to be. Liam shook her hand, smiling to mask his discomfort.

The man beside her shook his head, clicking his tongue, and stood. His shirt was half unbuttoned and his muscles flexed as he moved, his broad pectorals presenting neatly groomed chest hair.

'Aunt Adrienne, you're scaring the poor guy,' he said. 'Look, I know you know our name, but we're not here to cause trouble. We're here to protect you from the Cromwells. I don't know if you heard while you were sleeping next to your toilet, but they tore these streets apart.'

'Right. Protection.'

'Hey, I won't let anything bad happen to you.' The man sized Liam up and down appraisingly, then gave him a wolfish grin. He almost reminded Liam of Chad, what with the way he was comporting himself. 'I'm James.'

Liam shook his hand and they exchanged a few more pleasantries.

'Looks like I'll be working alongside you a lot,' said James. 'Victoria omitted to tell me this place has such a nice view.' He smiled and Liam felt himself blush – he was flattered. He awkwardly dismissed himself and got to work, cleaning and bussing tables and helping out at the bar.

* * *

After a few hours, James called Liam into the office where Victoria and Adrienne were discussing rosters.

'You asked to speak with me?' Liam said, poking his head in.

'Yes,' said James. He waved him in. Liam stepped into the office. 'We want to get to know you better.' He motioned towards the chair across the desk. 'Have a seat.'

Liam reluctantly sat down as Victoria dismissed herself. She paused, smiling at Liam. 'Chin up, you have to stop pining over that loser boyfriend someday.' Then she left.

'You have a boyfriend?' inquired James.

'No, not anymore,' replied Liam. It was partly the truth. 'He left.' That too was partly the truth.

'I'm sorry. I can't imagine why anyone would want to leave you,' said James, his tone sympathetic. 'You deserve better than that.'

'He means him,' Adrienne clarified, pointing a thumb at James, who spun his head to give her a pointed glare. Liam couldn't help but chuckle.

James redirected his gaze back to Liam. 'You have a lovely smile, Liam.'

Liam cleared his throat. 'Thanks. I'm certain Adrienne doesn't want to watch you flirt with me, so let's chat about whatever it is you wanted to talk about.'

Adrienne whooped out a laugh. 'I love your sense of humour.' She leaned forward in her seat. 'Listen, I know we can seem . . . well, we're a crime syndicate, we've been on the news, and we've got a reputation. The Cromwells are dangerous and we can keep this district safe from them. We want you to trust us, to feel safe around us.'

'And to keep my mouth shut when the cops come asking questions,' concluded Liam. 'I get it.'

'Good,' said Adrenne, though there was no threat in her tone.

'We also wanted to ask you about a former colleague who worked here a short while ago,' began James. 'The roster showed you had shifts with one Julian Lallard.'

Liam automatically clenched his jaw as his heart began to palpitate. He wondered if they were onto him and it took all his energy just to quell the impulse for his canines to extend and to keep his eyes from vampirically flaring and paling.

James shifted, his expression turning to one of sympathy. 'Oh, is that . . . I'm sorry, I hadn't realised he was the boyfriend who left.'

'I didn't say he was,' Liam clapped back.

'Your reaction gave it away,' Adrienne said gently.

'Has he come into contact with you?' asked James.

Liam tensed. He shook his head slowly. Could they tell if he was lying? They seemed rather astute.

'What does he have to do with you or the Cromwells, and why are you asking about him?' demanded Liam.

James hesitated. 'You see, this is going to sound crazy but . . .' Scooting his chair closer to the computer, he turned the screen around to show Liam. 'Have a look at this.'

'Is that a good idea, James?' Adrienne cautioned. 'Poor guy's stomach's been in shambles all week, you want to upset it even more?'

'He has to see this,' James insisted conclusively.

It was the footage of the night Julian saved Liam's life, the night Julian had returned. Liam was obscured by Julian shooting at the Cromwell vehicle with vampiric precision and speed.

'What am I looking at?' Liam asked, swallowing and trying to keep his breathing calm.

'Security camera footage from the night there was a shootout between us and the Cromwells,' explained James. 'Your ex is the one front and centre.'

'Yes, I can see that,' Liam said dryly.

'Notice how he's shooting?' asked Adrienne.

'Like he's got amazing skills to rival yours?' asked Liam, trying to sound unsure of his guess.

James chuckled. 'Sort of. We're not certain who the other man with him is, he's too obscured by Julian.' James paused. 'Liam,' he clasped his hands, leaning his elbows on the desk, 'there are forces of nature out there that don't want the rest of the world to know they exist, who wish to control the lives of others.'

Liam narrowed his eyes. 'Control?' As he said it, he realised he needed to control his anger. From what he knew of his new coven – and the vampires in general – was that control of humans was not what they wished.

Adrienne said pointedly, 'He's a vampire.'

Liam stared at her, then coughed. 'Vampires don't exist.'

'I understand your scepticism,' Adrienne said soothingly. She stood. 'Listen, this is a lot to take in. Perhaps we can continue this discussion later.'

'Wait.' James pondered for a moment, his fingers gliding along the long stubble on his chin. He clicked around on the computer and pulled up footage from a warehouse.

'This is from several months back,' he explained. 'Vampires attacking *our* warehouse.' He played the footage: Julian was fighting an armed security officer with speed, then his eyes flashed and paled, and then his canines extended and he bit into the man before tearing off his arm.

Clenching his jaw tight, Liam felt his body tense up, his pulse increased at an uncontrollable rate and his canines extended. He placed a hand to his mouth to cover it.

'I told you this was a bad idea.' Adrienne placed the small garbage can on the desk in front of Liam. 'If you're gonna be sick, do it in here and not on the floor.'

Liam merely nodded, taking a deep breath. He felt his canines retract, and he sighed in relief. He lowered his hand.

'So you want to expose the vampires?' Liam asked tentatively.

'Expose? You're joking!' exclaimed James. 'We want to eliminate them . . . *completely*.'

Liam stared at James and Adrienne, acutely aware of their guns, wondering how many silver bullets each had and what would happen if they discovered his true nature.

'Why?' he breathed.

'Because they pose a threat,' replied Adrienne. 'And we Sharpes have . . . history with them.'

This was the first Liam heard of any history between the Sharpes and the vampires beyond what he already knew, which was the vampires investigating the Sharpes and the Sharpes having knowledge of the vampires. He wondered if there was more to this than the elders had let on, than perhaps even Julian knew. Now was not the time to doubt his fiancé's veracity – Liam chose to trust Julian.

'What's it to do with the Cromwells?' asked Liam.

'The Cromwells know about them,' said James. 'They want to expose them. If that happens, chaos happens and we lose control as the leading mafia able to protect the city. We can't let that happen. Not to mention what can happen worldwide if that happens. No, we have to eliminate the vampires.'

'That is why,' Adrienne continued, 'if Julian ever gets in touch with you again, we need you to find out anything you can and we need you to lure him to us.'

Fear gripped Liam; he was not going to let these mobsters touch his fiancé. Julian was willing to protect Liam with his life – Liam felt the same way about Julian.

Liam merely nodded, staring at the garbage can in front of him, playing into the upset stomach act.

'Go on your break,' said Adrienne, sounding apologetic, 'and take it easy. Are you able to continue with the rest of your shift?' Liam nodded. She dismissed him.

Liam shut the door behind him, leaning his back against the wall next to the office, attempting to quell his fighting instincts. He heard James and Adrienne speak.

'We should have told him the full truth,' James sighed.

'Did you want him to actually be sick in here?' Adrienne scolded. 'We can't tell him. We can't tell anyone.'

So there was more to this – a bigger secret. Liam had to report this to Julian as soon as his shift ended.

* * *

For the next weeks, Liam played his role well and reported everything back to Julian and the others every time he learnt more. For his part, Julian didn't know about this history the Sharpes claimed to have with the coven, nor did the elders divulge anything to Liam if they *did* know anything.

Stella came into Nightly Glow every other night as a regular customer, keeping watch on the club and subtly letting Liam know she was there in case any trouble came his way.

As Liam had suspected, it was too dangerous to the mission for Julian to visit him, so they had to make do with video chats and phone calls. He missed him, but at least he knew he was safe. He insisted that Julian not come or fall for their trap, though Julian had claimed they would soon have to ensure he did walk into their trap as part of their plan. Liam hated that plan.

'Just like I hate the plan where I don't get to see you and you're right in the enemy's clutches,' Julian had retorted.

James kept flirting with Liam, and the fresh vampire played it up a bit, trying to get James to open up, perhaps spill whatever secret it was he had originally considered telling him. They had both confided in each other about some personal escapades they'd lived, and James seemed more than happy to talk about his bisexuality. However, nothing had yet been revealed to Liam regarding the secret the Sharpes concealed.

Now Liam stood in the office with James while on break as they chatted face to face – alone – the door closed behind them.

'I'm surprised your ex hasn't called you back yet,' said James, crossing his arms.

'Well, he was good at ignoring my calls before, no reason why he wouldn't return them now,' replied Liam. He bowed his head, his heart aching to be in Julian's arms again.

'Hey, you're not still pining over him, are you?' James lifted Liam's face with his fingers and stared Liam in the eyes. 'You deserve so much better than him, someone who'll care for you, protect you, someone who won't leave you.'

'Someone like you, you mean?' asked Liam, staring back into the man's brown eyes.

'Someone like me.'

James leaned closer, and for a moment Liam let him, considering his options. Their lips grazed, and at that moment Liam made his decision. He turned his head to the side, feeling his heart pulse faster. He missed these moments of intimacy with Julian, but he would not betray him with another man, not even for information.

'I'm sorry,' Liam whispered. He closed his eyes. 'I suppose I tend to go for the dangerous liars with secrets.' His gaze met James's once more.

James shifted his weight. 'Right.' He took a step back. 'There's something I need to tell you, something I've been meaning to tell you.'

Liam nodded carefully. This was it, he just felt it through his senses. 'Go on.'

'There's a reason why we want to eliminate the vampires, but why we don't want to expose them.' James hesitated.

Liam took a step towards him and tentatively took his hand. 'Look, I want to trust you, trust that . . . you're honest with me.'

James may have been a decade older than Liam but there was a vulnerability in his eyes Liam had never seen.

'Now that you know vampires are real, well, there are other beings that also exist.'

Liam's heart sank with dread.

'Liam,' said James, 'I'm a werewolf.'

Liam abruptly let go of James's hand and backed away from him. 'A *what*, now?'

'Listen, it's not what you think. We don't shift into humanoid wolves like in the movies, except once every full moon, you know, Feral Night, but, I mean . . . We just . . .'

Looking resolved, James extended his nails to form claws and his eyes became brighter, giving his brown eyes a golden-yellow glow. So the effect was similar to a vampire's. Liam did his best to quell his instincts in the manner he was briefly taught before he'd been plunged into the deep end of this whole plan.

'With control, we can make our teeth sharper and a bit more extended, though it's subtle compared to what happens to us on Feral Night.'

Liam thought about that for a moment. 'Never in the day, only at night?'

'We go feral from sundown to sunrise the night of the full moon,' explained James, perking up at Liam's curiosity, 'or whichever night is closest to the time the moon is full, before or after, if the moon is full in the day.' Liam supposed that made sense. 'Sorry,' James let out a laugh, passing his hand through his hair, 'it's been a while since I've had to explain this.'

'Right,' said Liam, staring at the werewolf, mouth agape, uncertain if the way James was looking at him meant he was trying to be flirtatious or cautious.

'We also have much longer life spans than humans, though we're not immortal like vampires are, nor are our lifespans as long as those of the fae folk,' explained James. 'My aunt's the Alpha. I'm a Sub-Alpha, nominated to be the next Alpha. There are other Sub-Alphas too, not just Sharpes. The Sharpes . . . we are the dominant family in the pack right now, but the pack is composed of many families, and it's our responsibility to ensure the pack's unity and safety.' He paused. 'Sorry, I know it's a lot to take in, but this is the truth that I've been meaning to share with you.'

'So that's why you want to eliminate the vampires,' Liam concluded. He knew there had been countless wars between the two kinds of beings but there hadn't been enough time for a full history lesson.

'Yes,' James answered. 'If they're exposed, we're *all* exposed. We don't want that. The Cromwells are onto them, we'll be next.'

'Then why not work *with* the vampires? Why not team up and take the Cromwells out together?!' insisted Liam.

'You don't understand, there is so much bad blood between vampires and werewolves.'

Liam chuckled mirthlessly.

'Our rivalry goes a long way back, you wouldn't understand.'

'Try me!' Liam demanded forcefully.

'It's always been the same thing repeated through history,' explained James, grit in his voice. 'Vampires killing werewolves, werewolves killing vampires, both factions out for the blood of the other for the atrocities done generations prior.'

'Who started it?' asked Liam.

'Who knows, really.'

'Then stop it, stop the feud. It might be hard at first, yes, but why blame the vampires of today for crimes committed centuries ago? Maybe some of them would be willing to set aside their grievances.'

'We tried that before, a very long time ago – there was a time when werewolves and vampires banded together and it only ended in more bloodshed for both factions,' James growled. 'No way are we trying that again. You'd be insane to think otherwise. It's how we're raised, to know our history, to know what was done to us. And because vampires are immortal, some of those alive today were alive back then too and are as responsible.'

'What about fresh vampires who never did anything to werewolves?' Liam argued.

'That fresh vampire would have to be one hell of a naive son of a bitch to think that we would cast aside millennia of bloody history between our factions!'

Liam couldn't argue against that. It would certainly help to understand their history to negotiate a truce. But both factions would have to set the past aside if there was to be any chance at that. Maybe Liam could do something to help that happen.

Liam fixed his gaze on James. 'What have the vampires of this city ever done to your pack?'

'Have you forgotten that your ex killed a member of my pack?' snapped James.

'Before that. Before they got involved with your pack and the Cromwells,' Liam clarified.

James turned his head to the side. When he spoke, his voice was heavy with woe. 'We can't just trust *any* vampire, Liam. The burden of honour to the pack and the *protection* of all the families that comprise the pack weighs heavily.'

James paused and met Liam's gaze once more, but this time there was a flicker in his eyes, one akin to a vampire's, and it quickened Liam's heart in apprehension. He realised werewolves could probably sense another's heart rate too, just like a vampire could, and Liam became acutely aware of James's fast-paced heartbeats.

Is a vampire's heart rate distinguishable from a human's or werewolf's? Liam knew that unlike in *some* stories, he *had* a heartbeat, but he hadn't had the time to learn if anything inside his body that a werewolf might detect would give him away if he failed to control his instincts.

He breathed in and out very slowly and very quietly as he attempted to quell the surge of fear that rose within him.

'Perhaps it *is* mere prejudice against vampires I never met,' James began carefully, 'but tell me this, *human*,' the over-emphasis raised the hairs on Liam's neck, 'who are you to advocate for vampires, when one of them lied to you and broke your heart while a werewolf stands before you baring his soul to you?'

They stared at each other for a long time, intensity growing by the second.

'I guess I'm just an idealist,' Liam offered, hoping it would quell the suspicion he sensed coming from James.

'Right.' James somewhat relaxed, but it was too late, Liam felt a prickle alert him to sudden danger and, even as he was careful to keep his mouth shut, his canines extended.

James was on top of him faster than Liam could react and, growling, the werewolf slashed his face with his claws before retreating.

Liam felt his eyes flare with power as he brought his hand to his face. Quickly, the gashes healed.

'You're one of them,' breathed James, disdain on his face.

Liam felt himself tremble as he and James stared at each other wide-eyed. Liam clenched his jaw and swallowed hard.

James's mouth hung open and he exhaled long, realisation dawning on his face. 'You're the other man in the security footage, the one obscured by Julian.'

'I'm the one who got shot, yeah,' Liam disdained. He placed his hand on his stomach. 'Julian saved my life.' James tensed his fingers. 'We don't have to fight, James, we don't have to be enemies. I don't know what the feud is, I've only been a vampire for a little over a month now, but I do know that if we put our differences aside, we can help each other.'

'It's a little too late for that,' growled James.

With a roar, he tore at Liam's shirt. Liam dodged with a speed he didn't know he had and grabbed James's arm, twisting it sideways as Wilbur had shown him. He kicked James away from him. James jumped up onto the wall, nails digging into the gyprock under the paint before lunging at Liam.

Liam moved aside in time but James was just as fast as a vampire. Liam bared his canines at the Sub-Alpha who roared again. The man came at him, ripping his shirt again. Liam let the damned thing fall to the floor.

James slashed him with his long claws and blood gushed from Liam's chest. He cried out, more in annoyance than pain as the adrenaline subdued the uncomfortable sensation before the wound healed itself.

Liam kicked James away again, not wanting to kill him, just wanting him to stop attacking him. He shoved so hard, James hit his head against the wall and a vase from the shelf above fell on him, shattering and causing little cuts on his hairy arms. Those cuts healed just as fast as Liam's wounds had.

James came forward again, arms raised and growling; Liam grabbed his arms and they pushed against each other.

'You lied, Liam!' shouted James. 'You're on a mission.'

'We didn't know the Sharpes were werewolves!' protested Liam.

'It doesn't matter. You're one of them and you lied, making me believe your pity story!'

James's eyes flashed again and this time his teeth sharpened, extending slightly. He was still in human form but it made his face more wolfish.

Liam knew if he bit the werewolf, he could either turn him, kill him, or incapacitate him, but he had not trained enough to know which was which. He still went for his neck, canines bared and ready to dig into his flesh, when the door to the office swung open.

Victoria stood on the other side of the threshold. They paused and pushed away from each other, panting. Liam turned his head to the opposite side, looking down at the ground, a hand on his mouth to give the semblance he was wiping his lips in order to hide his canines. James folded his arms and closed his hands into fists to hide his claws.

'You're going to have to postpone getting it on,' Victoria said grimly. 'We have company.'

She left, leaving the door wide open. There was shouting as clubgoers ran out of the club.

Liam and James looked at each other before they saw a tall bulky man walking around the club with at least a dozen others, armed and armoured for a fight.

'The Cromwells,' James hissed. He looked at Liam, face contorted in anger. 'This isn't over.'

'We can still work together,' insisted Liam. 'I don't see why we can't, especially now.'

They stepped out of the office to find everyone surrounded by Cromwell gang members; employees – humans and werewolves alike – remained unmoving and tense. The music was turned off and the place became quiet.

James and Liam made to join the group – a Cromwell trained her shotgun squarely on James and Liam as they slowly approached, the barrel steady and unwavering in her grip.

'Like I said,' the leader boomed, a tall man in a pinstripe suit, 'we're here to make a deal with you.'

'To hell with your deal!' snarled Adrienne.

'You like silver?' the leader asked Stella. 'Only you always wear gold jewellery. I hear you're allergic to silver.'

Adrienne swallowed loudly, even Liam heard it from where he was, now that his senses were heightened by adrenaline.

'Sharpes, we know you know about the vampires. We're willing to work with you to expose them.'

'We want them eliminated,' admitted Adrienne.

'Then eliminate her!' he pointed at Stella. 'We found two moles in our midst earlier today.'

'The twins,' Liam whispered.

'We just found you a mole, unless there is another you don't know about,' Cromwell went on. 'You Sharpes aren't as sharp as you think. You've got vampires in your midst working against you. We can help.'

'You want our help so you can then eliminate us,' complained Adrienne. 'This is war, Conrad, but the Cromwells didn't catch everything you think you did. We Sharpes *are* sharp.' Her nails extended and her eyes flared a bright yellow. 'The Cromwells and the vampires will perish.'

Around them, dozens of employees and patrons jumped towards the armed Cromwells, all of them werewolves.

James yanked Liam down to the ground with him as gunfire erupted throughout the club. Bullets whizzed past their heads, ricocheting off walls and shattering glass, their deafening roar reverberating through Liam's body. James shot repeatedly as the two sought cover from the chaos.

Liam quickly leaned towards James, muttering, 'Does silver kill werewolves too?'

'Yes,' growled James. 'Except we've got slightly higher tolerance levels than vampires do.' He swerved, avoiding a silver bullet.

'Meaning?'

He took aim and shot at a Cromwell lackey with quick precision. 'Meaning we stay conscious longer before it kills us.' James reflexively wrapped an arm around Liam and spun him out of the trajectory of a bullet whizzing past them.

'We need to work together, James!'

'Fine, but we're not done with our fight when this is over.'

'Fine!'

Remaining low, James kicked a table to its side and pulled it towards them to use as cover where they crouched. Gunfire tore through the club, and a bullet made of silver ricocheted off the metal table, sending a shower of sparks flying.

'Shit!' cursed James. He quickly ejected the magazine from his gun and fumbled for a new one.

Someone came barreling towards their makeshift hideout. Liam readied himself to pounce but James pushed him back down and shot the mobster in the chest, sending him to the floor.

'Stay down or you'll get yourself killed!' ordered James.

'What and do nothing?' protested Liam.

'You've been a vampire for a month, Liam, you hardly know how to avoid silver bullets, let alone—' He stopped to shoot at someone else.

Stella meticulously leapt towards another Cromwell member and tore her leg off. The woman shouted out before Stella dug her fangs into her.

'Fuck, she's fast!' James turned to Liam. 'Just, if we're working together, then we're working together.'

Adrienne and another werewolf tore at an enemy human, biting the flesh off vital parts of his body and leaving him to bleed to death.

Liam heard Stella bark orders at someone. 'It's going down *now!* Get your asses in here . . . NOW!'

Liam heard whimpering. He extended his senses. 'Victoria!' He leapt away from the safety of the upturned table and dashed with vampiric speed towards one of the V.I.P. rooms.

'Damnit, Liam!' shouted James. He leapt onto the wall, running along it with his claws and landed next to Liam in front of Victoria who huddled on the floor in a corner.

Liam crouched in front of her. She was shaking and tears streaked her face. The lovely woman suddenly looked so frail and fragile, curled into herself like that.

'I'm sorry you have to see all this,' Liam said gently.

She stared up at Liam. 'What's happening? I feel like I'm in a nightmare.' Liam reached out to take her hand and she recoiled in fear. 'Your eyes are glowing, they're, like, pale and weird.'

Liam bowed his head. 'I'm a vampire, Victoria.' Her eyes widened. 'I want to protect you.' She pointed behind him. Liam spun around in time to see two men launch themselves at James and him.

James tackled one to the ground and drove an elbow into his arm. The mobster dropped a knife Liam could sense was silver; it sparkled like glitter as it skittered across the floor. His heightened senses told him to duck, so he ducked. Liam grabbed the other man by the legs and sank his teeth into him. The man screamed and Liam sucked his blood – he hoped he was killing him. He cursed under his breath; he couldn't believe he'd just had that thought.

When both humans were dead, Liam turned back to Victoria, wiping his mouth with the back of his hand to remove the excess blood. Victoria looked pale, very pale. Then her eyes rolled to the back of her head and she fell unconscious.

'Probably for the better,' muttered James.

Liam scooped her up gently. 'We need to get her out of here.'

'Not so fast, vampire!' A werewolf landed before Liam as he turned to exit the room, blocking his path.

'Back off,' bellowed James. 'I'm handling him.'

'Of course, that's just like you to want to man-handle a good-looking guy, never mind that he's our enemy.'

'We're trying to work together here. In case you haven't noticed, the Cromwells are trying to kill us all.'

'Oh, I noticed. Except the fighting's out there and not in here!'

'Out of my way, werewolf,' demanded Liam, 'or I swear . . .'

'Or what?'

'Hey!' shouted James. 'Back off now, pup!' James growled and raised his hand, claws ready to strike the younger man. The werewolf deflated.

'All right, all right.' And with that, he ducked out of the room.

'Help me get her to safety,' Liam told James. Without waiting he exited the private lounge and dashed towards the back door through the corridor that led to it.

Before he could reach the club's exit, someone kicked it open.

'Liam!' shouted Julian.

Liam's eyes widened. 'Julian!'

Julian stood before him, blue eyes flaring with vampiric rage, shoulders hunched for combat. Behind him entered Chad, Mandy, Wilbur, and Richard, along with several others.

Julian's eyes immediately landed on Liam and his eyes widened.

'She's out cold but unharmed,' said Liam, running towards them.

Richard stepped forward. 'I'll get her to safety.'

'Richard.' Wilbur whispered something to him, and then the other vampire elder dashed so fast Liam could barely register his departure, even with his heightened senses and abilities.

Wilbur darted out of the corridor and into the club proper. Chad took a moment to listen to the sounds of the battle before nodding to Mandy. The ancient vampire's obsidian eyes flared and became a grey so pale they almost looked white, his pupils took on the colour of his irises, nearly as pale but darker still. He and Mandy dashed past Liam as several other vampires entered the club through the back exit.

Catching up and coming to a stop beside Liam, James glared at Julian. 'It's the boyfriend.'

'Fiancé,' both Liam and Julian corrected pointedly.

'Oh, sorry,' James retorted with sarcasm, lifting his arms in defence.

He stepped forward to block Julian's path as the other vampires dashed past the corridor to jump into the fray of the battle in the heart of the club.

Chapter Five

The werewolf sniffed Julian, giving him the most disdainful of sensations. 'Older but still fresh enough. I'm guessing roughly fifty years as a vampire, am I correct? We've been hunting you, although, thanks for taking out some of the Cromwells for us.' He turned to Liam. 'You sure know how to pick 'em. I still think I'm better for you.'

'What did you just say?' Julian put steel in his voice. It wasn't so much what the werewolf had said, but the way he had said it, almost implying—

No. Julian would trust Liam. He took in the sight of him again, feeling at once troubled and overjoyed to see him, though he felt wary as to why his chest was bare. A knot formed in his stomach, a knot of anger, and Julian clenched his jaw.

The werewolf chuckled. 'Relax, vamp, or do you think you can take on an Alpha?' He narrowed his eyes.

'I thought you said Adrienne was the Alpha and you were the Sub-Alpha!' Liam countered as Julian tried to push past James.

James placed a hand on Julian's chest to stop him. Julian grabbed his arm.

'Stop it, both of you!' Liam stepped between them. 'James, please, we're supposed to be teaming up right now.'

The sound of gunfire in the distance had become sporadic, but the fight was still ongoing beyond the corridor at the back where James, Liam and Julian were facing off. The occasional shout or growl echoed through the air, indicating that the battle was far from over.

'Thank me for protecting your newly turned vampire fiancé,' demanded James, 'and *taking care of him* while you were off doing whatever it was you were doing.'

'Planning to take your crime ring down until we learnt your syndicate was a pack,' seethed Julian, raising his fist; James grabbed Julian's wrist to stop him. They glared at each other, both flaring their eyes.

The vampires had learnt the news mere hours earlier and Julian had called Liam to warn him. Now he had to wonder why his fiancé wouldn't pick up. No – he pushed his doubts away. There were circumstances that would have prevented him from knowing Julian was calling.

Julian wrenched himself free from the werewolf's grip. 'No wonder you told Liam there was history between you and us.'

'Everything came to a head tonight,' concluded James, 'right when I was considering giving it.'

Anger flared within Julian. Who did this werewolf think he was? Even if none of it was true, Julian realised just how jealous he was. First of Chad, now of *this* guy? He hoped Liam wouldn't mind a possessive husband – part of him was so angry to be falling prey so easily to these ridiculous barbs.

'That's it, shut it!' bellowed Liam. James chuckled, licking his lips as Julian balled his hands into fists. 'Nothing of the sort happened. Stop taunting him, James.'

'So he knows, eh?' Julian said, staring at Liam.

'Yeah, he found out after he tried to . . .' Liam hesitated. 'He tried to kiss me.'

Julian snapped his head to James, ready to tear him limb from limb. 'You tried to kiss my fiancé?!' He glanced at Liam's shirtless chest and James's raggedly arranged clothes, unable to quell the doubt that rose within him. 'Unless you really did do more than—'

A table came crashing behind Liam at the far end of the corridor where it opened up to lead into the club proper, interrupting the argument between the two men. Julian reflexively ducked, as did James and Liam, before they realised no immediate threat followed.

Julian glared at James, slowly rising, his lips pulled back and baring his teeth, his anger pulsating from his core as his canines extended in a slow slick and threatening motion. 'You'll soon learn that if you touch my fiancé and hurt him, you die, just like the Cromwells who shot at him.'

'A little over-protective, aren't we?' James snorted, as he squared off against Julian once more. 'I'm not afraid of you, vampire!'

'Nor am I afraid of you, werewolf!'

Julian heard Liam curse as the two men lunged at each other, grabbing hold of each other's arms, Julian with his fangs out and mouth wide, trying to bite James, and James's claws extending even more as he tried to scrape flesh from Julian's face.

'You don't scare me – you're just a Sub-Alpha!'

James slashed at Julian who caught his arm, pushing back as they both exerted force. The werewolf was stronger than Julian had expected. He knew of the history between werewolves and vampires, centuries of war and rivalry, never in his life since he had turned did he think he would ever come face to face with one, let alone fight one – let alone fight one for the man he loved.

Julian turned James around and shoved him against the corridor wall.

Liam tried to get between them and ducked as James's fist came towards Julian's face. Julian blocked with the palm of his hand, pushing against the muscular man. He punched James in the gut. The werewolf staggered back before darting towards

Julian and slashing his arm. It stung but it would quickly heal.

Julian drew his arm back and his fist thrust forward, connecting with the werewolf's jaw. The Sub-Alpha retaliated in kind, following-through with his other fist and it struck Julian in the stomach. Winded, Julian grappled at James and the two held tightly against the other's arms.

Liam stepped towards them again, placing a hand on each of their shoulders. 'This is neither the time nor place for this.'

Julian and James were locked solid, neither willing to relent or let go of the other or stop pushing. Julian was intent on settling this once and for all. Both men growled, baring their teeth at each other – Julian his fangs and James his sharpened teeth.

Liam backed away from them hissing in frustration.

'I swear . . . if you laid one finger on my fiancé,' Julian threatened.

'Had I known you were so possessive, I wouldn't have waited to pounce on him!'

Julian shouted, putting all his strength against the other man. 'I'm going to end you!'

'Let's see you try. You're failing miserably *so far*.' James shoved against Julian with such force, the vampire staggered back, hitting his head on the wall behind him. 'We've been hunting you for a while now. You slaughtered members of my pack – it'll be an honour to be the one to claim this kill.'

Liam screamed in alarm and the intensity of it stilled Julian's heart. Both he and James stopped immediately and let go of each other.

Julian and James slowly turned their heads, their eyes widening in horror as they beheld Conrad Cromwell, resplendent in his navy pinstripe suit, holding his revolver – a revolver made of silver – to Liam's temple. The human clutched Liam as his arm draped around his bare chest, holding him firmly in place with a silver knife. The mere touch of silver would be enough to render Liam's powers useless if not knock him unconscious. A wide grin was plastered across the human's face, an unmistakable glint of sadistic pleasure in his eyes.

Julian froze, terror stilling his heart – it was happening all over again. He'd feared it would come to this, yet he got distracted by his petty jealousy. They were alone in the corridor and Liam was in danger because of Julian's anger. He could only blame himself.

Julian took a step forward and James stopped him.

'You'll get him killed.' James lowered his voice so only someone with heightened hearing could hear him. 'We need to coordinate and act strategically. We both agree we want him alive, yes?'

'Yes,' agreed Julian.

Julian stared, blinking back tears, fear rising within him. Liam looked so scared and vulnerable, he was trembling – Julian could sense him, smell him, and desperately wanted – needed – to protect him.

'Then how about we save him and then settle this once he's safe,' suggested James.

Julian conceded.

* * *

Liam felt like his heart was going to beat out of his chest with fear. Maybe he had always been meant to die, except this time it would be as a vampire, newly turned, with a silver bullet in his head.

The cold silver muzzle of Conrad Cromwell's revolver pressed against Liam's temple – the sensation was as though a block of ice was sticking to his skin. He could feel his body fighting against the silver gunpowder and against the press of the silver knife on his chest; surprisingly, the pain wasn't as intense as he had expected. He suspected it was because his fear was overpowering his physical sensations, too great for him to feel anything more. Yet, his body tingled as though it was instinctively healing the effects of the silver.

Liam saw and sensed the fear on Julian's face. James and Julian quickly glanced at each other and nodded.

Then the two pounced at the human with such speed, even Liam only perceived them as a blur. The revolver and knife were kicked from Conrad Cromwell's hand and went clattering to the floor. A fist tore through his abdomen as Julian landed a powerful blow to Cromwell's gut, yelling his rage.

Conrad Cromwell coughed blood, his eyes wide with shock. Julian pulled his arm out from the man's body and the human crumpled to the floor.

'You just took out Conrad Cromwell,' James breathed in disbelief.

'I did.' Julian's voice was guttural. It was filled with anger but somehow Liam couldn't help but feel a flutter of excitement – Julian had yet again saved his life.

'Let's deal with the Cromwells before we decide on doing anything else, okay?' Liam's breath was shaking.

Julian took a step towards Liam, reaching for his forehead in astonishment. He stopped himself before he would have smeared his face crimson, looking down at his bloodied arm. 'Thank god he didn't press hard enough to hurt you with the silver. You're a fast healer.'

Unable to answer, Liam stared at his fiancé, angry and yearning for him at the same time. 'We're going to have to talk about trust when this is over.'

Julian cast his head down in resignation and nodded.

'What do we do about *him?*' James asked abruptly, jerking his head towards the body.

'We claim victory against the Cromwells,' declared Julian.

He picked up Conrad Cromwell's body, draping him over his shoulder, and the three headed towards the main area of the club.

Lifting Conrad's body over his head as the dead man's blood plinked onto the floor, Julian called out, his voice cutting through the quieting fight and reverberating throughout the club. 'Your leader's dead! Give it up, mortals.'

He tossed the body and it landed with a loud thud and a splatter of blood. Everyone stared in shock. The quiet was disconcerting, it was as though no one dared react first.

'Looks like the vampires are useful for something.' James pointed a thumb in Julian's direction.

Everyone gaped at them. Julian grabbed a damp cloth from a nearby bar counter and wiped the blood off his arm.

'I killed Conrad Cromwell,' he announced. 'You have lost.'

'You heard him!' Wilbur shouted. 'Your leader is dead. Now give up the location of your main base of operations and we'll give you a clean and merciful death.'

'Holy shit, Julian,' shrieked Mandy. 'You did a good one for us there!'

Julian smiled meagerly. Then he gaped longingly at Liam as everyone scrambled to finish off the remaining Cromwell fighters.

Liam let out a breath. 'Thank you for saving me – again – my fiancé.' He smiled.

Julian closed the distance between them and grabbed hold of his arms. He stared at him with such intensity Liam felt like everything around them was fading from view, and all sounds became muffled, as everything around them calmed and settled. The world only existed for them now.

Julian pressed his lips to Liam's, sending tingles vibrating through Liam's body. He held him tightly.

'I thought I was going to lose you all over again.'

'Julian,' Liam pulled away. 'I'm all right.' Liam placed his hand on his face. 'As for James . . .' He shook his head.

A body landed on the table right next to them and they bounced away reflexively, lunging to the floor for cover, before realising everything was quiet and the fight seemed to be over for good. Not far, James was also on the floor in a half-crouch, alert and ready.

'Clear!' Stella shouted.

'Any news from Zack and Zanitha?' asked Chad, as he strode towards her.

'They'll have gone underground,' replied Stella. 'Last time someone declared them dead, you remember the stunt they pulled. I expect they'll lie low for a while. Don't let it worry you.'

Liam barely knew them but he hoped they were all right, as Stella assumed.

The other vampires and werewolves began cleaning the mess around the club.

'Gather all necessary items,' Adrienne barked. 'We're going to have to vacate.'

Liam sat up, still catching his breath. Julian sat up beside him. 'You okay?'

'Yes, I'm fine.'

'I'm fine too, thank you for asking.' James propped an elbow on his knee. He and Julian glowered at each other.

'Julian!' Liam said firmly. 'I'm yours.'

Julian returned his gaze to Liam. 'I . . . I'm sorry I doubted you. But he tried to kiss you! I just get so jealous.'

'I know, it's part of why I love you, it's how I accept you,' Liam reassured him. 'But I need you to trust me.'

'I know – I'm sorry.' Julian and Liam smiled gently at each other.

'Always go for the single ones,' Chad chided playfully. He offered his hand to James, who took it, and helped him up. Chad grinned, sizing James up and down. The two of them appraised each other properly, and something passed between them – they both looked awestruck. 'I'm Chad, by the way. And single.'

'James Sharpe. And on the prowl.' The two smiled from ear to ear at each other.

Julian and Liam laughed, and let themselves fall back onto their backs.

Liam took Julian's hand in his and turned his head to look at him. 'Things just got so much more complicated after I turned, didn't it . . . and a lot simpler too.' They laughed again.

Leaning towards each other, they kissed, ignoring everything else around them. Liam flipped on top of Julian, placing a hand on the floor beside Julian and rubbing up against him, not caring if they had an audience or not, only wanting Julian.

Chad muttered something to James before they removed someone's body from the floor nearby. Liam chuckled onto Julian's lips, focusing his hyper senses on him alone. A muffled Stella barked another order.

Julian wrapped his arms around Liam's bare back and pulled him closer to him. He spoke between heavy kisses. 'I think . . . they could . . . use . . . our help.'

'I don't care,' Liam whispered gruffly. 'I want you, and I want you now.'

In response, Julian opened his mouth to take Liam's lips in, sucking them into his mouth and gently grinding his teeth onto them. The sensation tickled Liam's senses and he reflexively grabbed Julian's hand, interlacing their fingers.

Between heavy kisses, Liam expressed, 'I want you, Julian; I want you so fucking bad I can't control myself.' He pressed his lips to Julian's and plunged his tongue into his mouth before lifting his face to moan, 'I need you . . . now!' The last part came out as a growl.

'That'll be your primal instincts kicking in.' Julian's eyes flared and Liam could feel the other vampire's desire just as strongly as his own, he could feel his lover's heartbeat as though it were in his chest, and he could hear his breath like it was his own.

Liam became acutely aware of how quiet the club was, now that everyone had left. He grinned. 'We have the place all to ourselves.'

Julian looked to the side. 'They even got rid of all the bodies for us.'

'I never would have imagined making love to you on the floor of Nightly Glow Club after a vampire-werewolf mafia shootout, let alone wanting to.' Liam felt his eyes flare. 'I just want to ravage you.'

'That'll be the vampiric adrenaline pumping,' grinned Julian.

'No, it's my love for you pumping in my entire body.' To emphasise, Liam rubbed his pelvis against Julian's, letting his lover feel his erection through their clothes just as he felt Julian's.

Julian glided his hand along Liam's chest, pressing against his pectoral. He let out a guttural sigh. 'We need to stop doing this, going a whole month before we can devour each other's bodies again.'

Liam chuckled, continuing his sliding motion as he lay on top of Julian.

'Oh Liam, you feel so good!' Julian lifted his pelvis to press it up against Liam's, sending a surge of arousal through his body.

Julian undid Liam's belt, pulling on it and tossing it aside. Digging into Liam's pants, Julian grabbed hold of Liam's erection.

'Oh, fuck, yeah,' breathed Liam.

Straddling Julian, Liam crawled closer and angled his erection so Julian could take him deep into his mouth. Julian tickled Liam's shaft with his tongue, teasing him. Liam moaned his need. Julian obliged and nearly swallowed Liam's cock, so deep did he suck it in.

'Oh yeah, oh Julian. Oh fuck, Julian!' Liam already felt inebriated. His hands reached up to grab the table that stood in his midst to find purchase as his body convulsed with pleasure.

Julian pulled him out. 'Fuck Liam, you taste so fucking good.' He plunged him deep into his throat again and Liam let out a euphoric cry. He felt Julian's canines glide along the sides of his cock, adding to the already exuberant sensation pulsating from his pelvis.

'Fuck, Julian, that feels amazing.'

In response, Julian sucked harder and Liam began to sweat more as the room around him spun. He bucked his hips, jerking his head back and shouting. He lowered his arms and grabbed Julian's shoulders hard as his cock plunged deeper again and again into the other vampire's throat.

'Fuck, yeah!'

Reaching behind him, Liam undid Julian's pants and reached inside. He gripped Julian's cock, placing his fingers so he could fondle Julian's perineum as he stroked him – his lover's cock was so smooth, he could tell Julian was freshly shaved. Julian was already seeping – hard and ready. Liam played with him as Julian continued to suck him. Julian moaned onto Liam's cock and the vibration sent him over the edge. Erupting into Julian's mouth, Liam screamed as his orgasm culminated.

Liam pulled out of Julian's mouth and sank lower, gripping his lover's cock hard and taking it into his mouth right before Julian spilled into it. Julian slammed a fist onto the floor, swaying his head this way and that as he shouted out in ecstacy. Liam continued to suck – he wasn't done.

He felt Julian build up again, panting heavily and groaning, his erection stiffening. At the last second, Liam slipped it out of his mouth, pulled his lover's pants off and lifted Julian's legs, pushing his knees towards his chest – Julian encouraged him by adjusting the position. Liam spat on his hand and rubbed his saliva on his cock before teasing his fiancé's entrance.

Julian let out a moan of anticipation and Liam remembered the lube. He reached into Julian's pants and got the tube out.

'Now are you happy I have that on me?' Julian breathed huskily.

Liam didn't answer but grinned at him seductively as he lathered his cock just enough, his shaft always resting on Julian's hole. Grabbing hold of Julian's ass cheeks, Liam inserted himself into his lover's rectum.

'Oh my god!' he screamed – Julian felt so good. Gripping Julian's cock anew, Liam stroked vigorously as he pumped himself into Julian's ass. The momentum mounted once more, and for a long echoing moment, both men screamed into the empty club.

'Fuck!' shouted Julian. 'God, this feels good!'

He spilled all over his stomach as Liam's elation calmed. Liam pulled out gently and bent to lick

Julian's naval clean, gliding his tongue from the man's pelvis to his belly button, and flicking his tongue before going down again and licking his way up again. He licked all the way up to Julian's mouth and devoured his fiancé's lips, sucking in his tongue and lips. He was still getting used to feeling their long canines with his tongue and it pumped his arousal so much.

'I just can't get enough of you,' he said in a husky voice.

Julian chuckled, still panting. 'Well, I think I'm all pumped out for now, so we're going to have to give it a few.'

'Awww shucks!'

Liam laughed and allowed himself to rest on top of Julian for a few minutes. Then, the two lovers reluctantly pulled away from each other, lifting themselves off the floor. They retrieved their clothes and walked over to the employee washroom to clean up before dressing and exiting the club.

Chapter Six

Julian crossed his arms, feeling awkward in Liam's cramped apartment as vampires and werewolves argued about snacks.

After the ordeal at the club, the beings had vacated the premises to give Liam and Julian the privacy they needed for the intimacy they were claiming no matter who was around to watch or overhear. When Julian and Liam exited the club, they found everyone outside, waiting for them as though nothing was.

They had argued over where to hold a meeting. The club was too conspicuous – they needed to clear out and stay away for a bit, thus it was a no-go. Despite agreeing on this, neither group had wanted to divulge the location of any of their safehouses, let alone their main bases of operation. Thus Liam had offered his apartment.

Julian and James had discussed their differences on the way there.

'I understand you didn't know you were killing werewolves,' James offered as they walked side by side.

'Knowing the history between our kinds – let alone the fragile line between coexisting and outright war – I would have thought twice about striking a retaliating blow,' Julian responded. 'I understand your fury with me. I know sorry isn't going to cut it.'

'They weren't Sharpes,' said James, 'but they were trusted members of the pack.' He sighed, passing a hand through his hair. He glanced at Liam, then at Chad, who walked a few paces ahead of them, before returning his attention to Julian. 'I recognise that to you, you were fighting for the survival of the vampire kind and you thought we were no different from the Cromwells. From an outsider's perspective, that's what we are – rich mobsters who own half the city.'

James faced front again. 'Listen, we don't kill needlessly. We're *not* like the Cromwells. We own businesses, we make money through *mostly* legitimate means, but we're werewolves, and we protect the pack no matter what and eliminate our threats through the smartest means possible.'

Julian took that in, acknowledging.

James pursed his lips. 'That night, my pack mistook you for a Cromwell. I get that you were fighting for your life.' He met Julian's gaze, his expression unreadable.

'Your people attacked me,' Julian confirmed.

'The security footage showed us you were one of the vampires from the coven we sought to . . . investigate.'

'I was doing reconnaissance – I had no intention of fighting that night,' Julian admitted. 'I did what I had to but that doesn't mean that now, in light of our new situation, I don't regret it.'

'Look, before that night, your coven and my pack never exchanged blows, and if we don't work together now and set aside our grievances, then both the vampires and werewolves of this city and surrounding suburbs risk extermination. I get that. I don't know how the Cromwells got their Intel, but what we've learnt about them irks me.'

James looked up ahead at Liam and Chad – it sounded like Chad was instructing Liam in more combat techniques.

'I learnt at a young age to hate all vampires, but what Liam said to me earlier . . .' He exhaled.

'And I learnt to be wary of werewolves from the moment of my turning,' replied Julian. 'But today was the first time that I knowingly faced one.'

James paused and watched as Chad nudged Liam with his elbow, the vampire elder glanced back and smiled. Julian stopped beside him.

'Perhaps it *is* time I set aside my prejudice and started fresh,' admitted James, 'with vampires who never wronged me, and maybe we'll find common ground enough to discover we can truly coexist. Perhaps we don't have to hold onto the past and walk that precarious tightrope where one wrong move reignites a war of centuries ago.'

They resumed. Chad and Liam slowed to let them catch up.

'I'm certain you'll discover you don't hate *all* vampires.' Chad winked at James, a devilish smile on his face.

James chuckled, averting his eyes. 'Then perhaps you can show me how much of an asset you and your coven can be in alliance with my pack against the Cromwells.'

'Oh, I can show you *all* my assets, James.' Chad offered James his hand. 'You just need to take a leap of faith – some of us have already made the first move.'

James accepted Chad's outstretched hand, and with fingers interlaced, they followed Liam and Julian up the stairs to the apartment, with the other coven and pack members right behind them.

Now everyone was hungry, cranky, and no one was agreeing on what to do next. The only ones not arguing were Chad and James, who instead were flirting with each other. At least James was moving on from wanting Liam, which Julian preferred.

Now, aside from the vampires needing to hunker down for the day, the apartment windows having been boarded up, the issue was how had the Cromwells figured out there were vampires near their territory?

Based on what both the vampires and the werewolves revealed, it seemed there had been a leak –

something or someone had reached the Cromwells and shown them proof of vampire existence. The questions were how and when, and most importantly, who and why.

A loud knock on the door interrupted everyone's arguing. Liam closed his eyes, sighing in his throat. He made a beeline for the door, his hand gesturing to Stella to holster her weapon as she trailed behind him with her gun at the ready.

When Liam opened the door, a middle-aged woman in a housecoat and slippers stood on the other side.

'Rent's due!' She poked her head in. 'And what did I say about parties?'

'We're not a party,' said Liam.

'Of course, you're not.' She sounded unconvinced.

'We're vampires and werewolves,' said Chad, grinning.

'Of course,' the landlady condescended to Chad. She turned her head back to Liam, waving her finger about as she spoke. 'Well, when you and your friends are done roleplaying, bring me my rent.'

'Will do,' replied Liam.

The woman shuffled away and Liam shut the door.

Mandy slapped Chad on the arm.

'Ow!'

'Do you have to be such an idiot?'

'She didn't take me seriously!' protested Chad. 'Dude! Sometimes the best defence is the truth.'

'Whatevs,' Mandy replied with a giggle.

Julian observed how the vampire elders seemed a lot more agreeable to cooperating with the werewolves than the other way around, but at least someone was willing to make the first move.

'All right, suppose we agree to this,' said Adrienne, 'we need a plan of attack. While I don't like the idea of working with vampires, I concede that we're going to need to put our feud aside, at least for one night.'

'The Cromwells didn't know their rival gang was in fact a pack of werewolves until last night,' said James. 'Now that they know, they'll be doubling down on their attacks with the silver weapons – bullets, knives, you name it. We need to hit them before they have a chance to regroup.'

'We've hit them where it hurts,' said Julian. 'I've killed Conrad Cromwell, their leader. We retain an advantage right now.'

'Still, they must have sub-leaders and co-leaders, much like you vampires and we werewolves do,' countered James. 'As you know, my aunt is the chosen Alpha,' he pointed towards Adrienne. 'If she is eliminated, the pack will not fall into disarray. First off, her husband is the Partner-Alpha.'

An older man with a well-kept beard and curling moustache raised his hand and waved. 'That would be me, Martin Sharpe.'

'I'm the preferred Sub-Alpha,' continued James, 'though there are a few in competition with me. If I am chosen to be the Alpha, my partner would be the Partner-Alpha, and would have just as many responsibilities towards the pack as I do. And the Sub-

Alphas are there not just as contenders for a future leadership role but to take charge should anything happen to both the Alpha and the Partner-Alpha.'

Now Julian understood where he was going with this.

'Hence, no matter what happens to me or anyone of the Alphas, there are others who can take their place immediately and know what to do in the event of an emergency, to reorganise, regroup, and retaliate. Hence, the Cromwells are regrouping as we speak. We need to strike while the iron is hot.'

'Unfortunately, since vampires can't make it longer than a couple of hours in the sun before our insides literally melt,' began Wilbur, 'we can't proceed until night falls.'

'Thankfully, however,' Stella pointed out, 'we are in the middle of Winter and night falls early.'

There was a pause.

'What if we hit them during supper?' suggested Martin Sharpe. 'Catch them unawares.'

'Agreed. We need to hit them as early as possible,' Adrienne declared.

'I have no objections,' said Stella.

'Neither do I,' Chad concurred.

'Then we know what we must do,' said Wilbur.

* * *

The host of vampires and werewolves crept towards the lavish mansion wherein lived the Cromwells. It was a gaudy house in a gaudy district, with three driveways and more cars than was necessary for a family to own. At least the coven manor had that elegant Renaissance appeal to it, Liam thought. This was just over-the-top flexing.

Liam and Julian waited, huddled beneath a window. Then, Adrienne gave the signal with a guttural roar Liam didn't know the woman could do.

At once, vampires and werewolves alike stormed the mansion, crashing in through windows and slamming into the Cromwells as glass shattered around them.

Liam saw Chad rip the arm off one man, while Stella twisted her opponent's neck, snapping him dead. Wilbur and several other vampires were on top of the headmistress of the Cromwell family, while werewolves were baring their teeth and biting into the human fighters and bodyguards. The strong humans were overpowered by the muscular werewolves and went down one by one as the walls were painted red with their splatter.

Mandy and a small group of vampires leapt towards another room, taking out more Cromwell lackeys.

Liam, Julian and James headed towards the back of the mansion, looking for the armoury, as they had been tasked to do. Carrying a fire launcher on his back, James bounded forward like a beast, propelling himself on the walls to go faster, while the vampires used their vampiric speed.

They came to a halt before a large metal door that looked distinctly like the door to a safe. It glittered beneath the light in the hall.

'Lined with silver,' panted James. 'Should have guessed.' He took a few steps back, observing the door. 'It's a crude lining, just enough to ward off us beings of the Underworld.'

'We need a way in,' claimed Julian.

James flashed him an annoyed glare. He kicked the door handle as hard as he could with a resounding thud from his boot. It bent.

James inclined his head to the side. 'It's a start.' He kicked it again, and again.

A bullet whizzed past Liam's head and he moved just in time to avoid it.

'Cover me!' bellowed James.

Liam and Julian leapt towards their attackers, ripping off limbs and plunging their fangs into their necks to kill them. Even if Liam hadn't had full training yet, Chad had told him if he pulled on the artery, he would guarantee a kill rather than accidentally turn a human. So that's what Liam did, pulled arteries with his fangs to ensure the mobsters were dead.

Finally, James kicked the handle off and the door clicked open. Kicking the door open with his boot, the werewolf lunged into the room.

'Time to melt these babies!' he roared. He hoisted the fire launcher from his back onto his shoulders.

'Are you sure that thing's hot enough?' asked Liam. 'And are you sure that thing won't melt *with* the silver?'

'Come on, it's been designed specially for this. This is titanium steel, baby! And silver melts at one K Celcius.'

'Shit!' Liam breathed.

'And we can take it,' James grinned. Liam would have to ask about that later.

The launcher roared as it blazed, and the heat around them rose as the silver weapons began to liquefy. Liam felt like he was in a sauna as sweat beaded on his skin, making his long bangs stick to his face.

The silver pooled on the floor. James stopped the fire launcher, now a fiery red around its nozzle.

'Might not stop them in the long run, but it'll slow them down while we take them out,' said James with a satisfied grin on his face.

Backing up and out of the safe, James let the fire melt the door's lining until there was no more fire coming from the launcher. He cast the launcher aside, the sound echoing in the hall – an echo that should have been drowned out by the sounds of fighting.

Julian looked around. 'It's too quiet.'

'Fighting's moved outside,' noted Liam. He could hear shouts coming from the back of the mansion.

The three of them headed for the exit.

'There you are!' Chad sighed in relief as he arrived from an adjacent corridor. 'We've got company.'

That's when Liam heard the sirens.

'Great,' growled Julian, 'the last thing we need is cops on our tail on top of the Cromwells.'

'This way!'

Chad led the group out to where the fighting had moved. Many Cromwell members lay dead on the terrain, but so did several werewolves and vampires. The four of them were still close to the mansion when they noticed the fighting had moved towards the cliffside treeline that led to the river shoreside.

Liam readied himself to use his speed when James put a hand out to stop him. 'Wait.' James pulled Liam down with him behind a hedge. Chad and Julian crouched beside them.

'Wait?' argued Liam.

James sniffed the air. 'I smell—'

'We have to go help them!'

'No, look.'

Liam followed James's gaze – in the surrounding evergreens, there were glints of officers in camouflage and black armour.

'This isn't a quickly put-together team of cops coming to stop a commotion,' observed Chad.

'It's a whole fucking SWAT team,' Julian disdained.

'The fire launcher must've dampened the sound of the sirens before the fighting moved,' noted Liam. 'Unless . . .' He didn't like where his train of thought was leading him.

'They're way too organised,' remarked James. 'Sirens to lead the groups to scramble out back, SWAT team to take them out.'

'Shit!' hissed Chad.

The four crept along behind the hedges, looking for a way out without being spotted.

'I suppose going back inside the mansion is out of the question?' asked Liam.

As if in response, gunshots and shouting erupted from inside the mansion, the unmistakable voices of the SWAT team ringing out in the din.

'I guess not.'

One of the officers out back took aim, signalling the others, and then they opened fire . . . on both the Cromwells and the Underworld beings, creating instant carnage.

'Oh my god!' breathed Chad.

A vampire went down near them, a dark inky asterisk-shaped wound spreading across her neck.

Julian bristled. 'They've got silver bullets. They know, the cops know.'

'Shit!' cursed James. 'Someone sold us out!'

'If we don't move from here, they'll find us, and then we're done for,' snapped Chad.

'The roof,' James barked.

He thumbed a grenade and tossed it far towards the trees, the explosion was enough to blind anyone. In the darkness that followed, the vampires leapt up to the roof in one sprint, while James scaled it in quick bounds.

From the roof they had a better vantage point and could see who was escaping and who was down. They lay flat on their stomachs, unable to do more. Liam felt helpless.

'We can't stay here all night,' hissed Julian.

'We have to wait till things calm, though,' countered Chad. He cursed under his breath. 'If I hadn't come back to look for you . . .'

'Then you'd be among the dead,' Julian whispered harshly. 'There's nothing you could have done for them.'

Chad looked tormented. He tore his gaze away from the carnage, shutting his eyes as vampires died below. James stared in shocked dismay, fists clenched so tightly they were trembling.

Heart palpitating, adrenaline coursing through their bodies, they waited until it was safe to come down. The cops had left, and anyone still alive was long gone. The moon was still up, but they needed to get somewhere safe soon.

They walked amidst the bodies. 'My god,' breathed Liam, feeling his stomach rise to his throat. He'd seen carnage earlier that night – and had contributed to it – but this was something else. The dead humans were like any other human shot in various areas of the body, blood pooling beneath them in the snow, but the vampires and werewolves looked tormented, faces frozen in agony, and their skin infected, with black tendrils snaking from the wounds.

'That's what silver does to us,' explained Chad. 'A non-fatal wound takes more time to take effect but if it spreads – it's worse than being caught in the sun.'

'Is death certain?' asked Liam.

'Not always,' replied James. 'Depends where the bullet hits – or whatever weapon is used. Sometimes, if tended to in time, a werewolf or vampire, or fae for that matter, can be saved. But the minute silver enters the bloodstream, we don't have much time before it's too late.'

Liam swallowed hard as he stared at the contorted and torn bodies. 'Any sign of the other elders and leaders?' he asked.

'Not that I've seen,' replied Julian.

James stopped, staring down at one of the dead on the ground, his jaw tight.

'A pack member,' Chad surmised, speaking gently.

James nodded. 'She was a contender and rival of mine, another Sub-Alpha. We had a lot of respect for each other. She was . . . a friend.'

'I'm sorry.' Chad took James's hand.

James closed his eyes, turning away from the scene. His face was close to Chad's and when he opened his eyes, emotions flickered between them. Chad had a remarkably solemn look on his face Liam had not seen before, and his voice was filled with sadness.

'I know what it's like to lose those for whom you care.'

James blinked back tears. 'Let's get out of here,' he growled.

The click of a gun's hammer stopped them in their tracks.

'Not so fast!'

Liam's heart raced. The group whirled around to stand facing a man who looked like a twenty-year-old version of Conrad Cromwell.

'Which one of you killed my father?' he demanded, seething.

His hands were smeared crimson, blood streamed down the side of his face, but he looked otherwise alive and ready to kill. And he was pointing his gun directly at Liam. His trigger finger twitched nervously as he aimed the gun at Liam's head, betraying his trembling rage.

Julian was on top of him in no time. He twisted the young Cromwell's arm upwards as a shot from his gun tore through the night. He kicked Cromwell to the ground, baring his fangs.

Julian twisted the young Cromwell's head, plunging his fangs into the man's neck before coming up and leaping away as more gunshots filled the air, silver bullets speeding towards them.

'Shit!' cried James. 'Run!'

The four of them dashed through the trees, dodging bullets as best they could.

Chad spun around, firing his gun at the mobsters, quickly taking down three of them with three successive shots. Despite not yet having learned to use a gun himself, Liam couldn't help but admire the ease with which the others dispatched their targets. James followed suit, taking quick aim with his gun and eliminating four more. Only three mobsters remained.

Chad jumped over some underbrush as the three vampires and one werewolf continued to run. They halted suddenly when they came to the thorn-brambled overhang, assessing which way they should go or if the jump down was too far even for them.

James pointed down at the riverbank, indicating a path to take, before they were under fire again, bullets whizzing past their ears, their sound amplified by vampiric senses.

The four beings sprang to one side, heading towards the sloping path, ready to leap down.

A bullet landed in flesh, and Julian went down, falling off the edge of the cliff.

CHAPTER SEVEN

A bullet landed in flesh, and Julian went down, falling off the edge of the cliff.

'Julian!' screamed Liam, feeling like his heart was being torn apart.

He spun to face the three men approaching them, bloodthirsty rage rising within him. He roared, baring his fangs at them, his hot breath forming a cloud in the freezing twilight, and he leapt towards them, letting his vampiric instincts guide him.

He grabbed one by the neck and yanked his hair hard, beheading him – warm droplets splattered Liam's face. He slammed this one's head into another's face before he brought his fang down into his neck and tore the flesh from it, pulling veins out as blood streamed everywhere, the metallic smell rising to his nostrils.

The third froze in place, hands shaking as he held his gun with both hands, and Liam punched his gut, tearing through skin and muscle, ripping the man's insides and pulling them out. Liam watched as this last one crumpled to the ground beside the other two.

Liam stared at the carnage he had created on the red-speckled snow, trembling with rage. Part of him felt sick at the thought that he was capable of doing this, that he *had* done this. Another part of him didn't care.

His vision blurred with tears, Liam spun and leapt from the edge of the cliff. He landed next to Julian's limp form and fell to his knees. His fiancé had landed on a patch of grass, flat on his stomach – his hand on his arm indicated Julian had been conscious long enough to attempt to remove the bullet himself before he succombed to the silver poisoning. Liam gently turned him over onto his back.

Julian was still breathing. Liam's breath caught in his throat – Julian was alive!

Liam sobbed loudly, tears pouring down his face, holding Julian close, now unable to contain his grief and fear, not knowing what to do.

Chad and James approached him – someone placed a hand on his shoulder.

'He's alive.' Chad knelt beside Liam and lifted Julian's blood-drenched arm. 'It's enough to knock him out cold. If we can get the bullet out and give him some blood, he can survive this.'

A small ray of light scintillated on the horizon.

'But we need to get out of here, Liam,' Chad continued gently.

Liam shook his head, weeping. 'I'm not leaving him.'

'We're not leaving him, we're taking him with us,' Chad reassured. 'We need to go someplace safe.'

'We've been compromised,' James warned. 'Cops were too organised, they went after everyone, and they had silver bullets. There's got to be a mole somewhere. Safehouses aren't safe until we hear from our leaders.'

'I thought you *were* a leader,' retorted Chad.

'I am, but I'm not the one at the top. You've got your leaders too! You're an elder but you vampires operate with recognised authority from a select few. From what I understand, you've chosen to be a Sub-Alpha in your own respects, no matter how ancient you are. That puts both of us at a disadvantage – we *have to wait* to hear from our leaders.' He took a beat. 'What's your coven's protocol?'

'Lie low and call no one, wait until the chosen leading elders call you,' replied Chad.

'Then we need a place where we can do just that.'

Liam could hear them, but all he could do was hold Julian close to his chest protectively, unable to move anymore.

'Liam,' Chad began gently, 'we need to get out of here. In a few hours, we'll be dead if we stay out in the sun.' He paused.

Liam heaved.

'We need to leave, Liam, and we need to leave now.' His voice was firm but compassionate.

'Where the hell are we going to go?' demanded James. 'We need to figure out where we can go.'

Liam looked up at them. 'I know where.'

He stood, scooping Julian up into his arms. 'Keep up or fall behind, it's up to you.'

With that, he tore off, dashing forward. The rising sun stung his skin, as though he had spent hours outside on the hottest day of Summer. It burnt, it hurt, he felt itchy sores begin to welt on the exposed parts of his skin – so this was what it felt like.

He could sense Chad and James behind him. The werewolf, for his part, was able to keep up, though Liam suspected Chad was helping him dash, for vampires did move at a more rapid pace, let alone an elder's speed being unrivalled.

Liam raced furiously towards the familiar neighbourhood in the suburbs – careful to take roads where he knew no one would see them dart past at such speed – and to the bungalow he knew. He hammered on the door, calling out.

'Rachel! Rachel, are you in? Come on, Rachel, let me in.'

'Okay, okay! Geez.' Rachel opened the door – it was a relief to see her. Her dark green eyes widened in shock. 'My god, Liam, what happened? You're covered in blood!'

'I'll explain later. Julian's hurt.' Liam pushed past Rachel, carrying Julian into his old bedroom which now served as a guest bedroom – it was a room on the shady side of the house, so it would do.

'You mean, the Boyfriend-Who-Left-You Julian?' Rachel called after him as she followed him to the room.

'He didn't leave me! And he's my fiancé now.' Liam delicately set Julian down on the bed.

'You mean to tell me you got engaged and didn't even bother to call your sister to tell her!?'

'I need your tweezers, a wet cloth, and . . .' He faltered. He wavered a bit in place before his strength gave way and Liam fell to his knees. Chad helped him up, looking just as weak.

Liam turned to Rachel. 'Do you have steak or . . .' He stopped, breathing heavily.

'I've got some liver in the fridge,' Rachel replied, sounding unsure.

'Yes, that! Get the blood in a glass, please.'

Rachel looked from Liam to Chad to James and then Julian. 'Okay, whatever you and your friends are into now, don't let me stop you.'

'Rachel, just . . . please, I'll explain everything after.'

She lifted her hands in surrender. 'Okay, okay.'

Rachel left and Chad closed the drapes in the room, ensuring no sun seeped in from anywhere, casting the room into semi-darkness.

'Had we been out there any longer, we would have needed human blood,' said Chad, his breathing laboured. He looked down at Julian, coming to sit on the bed on the opposite side. 'That is what Julian will need if he is to survive.'

Liam nodded, understanding Chad's meaning.

It didn't take long before Rachel returned with the animal's blood in a small glass. Liam took a few swigs and gave the rest to Chad. Already he felt his strength returning and the itch on his skin subsided. Chad's welts began to fade and the elder vampire sat straighter.

Liam sighed. He looked at his sister. 'Thank you.'

Eyes wide and looking puzzled, she handed him her eyebrow tweezers and a couple of damp cloths, one for Julian's wound and the other for Liam to wipe his hands clean. He took them and sat down on the bed opposite Chad as the elder vampire took the tweezers from him.

'Hold his arm like this,' instructed Chad, cupping his hands.

'My god,' exclaimed Rachel as she drew closer, 'that wound looks terrible.'

Liam ignored her. He held Julian's arm – Chad dug in with the tweezers, pulling out the silver bullet. Julian gasped haggardly, his eyes shooting open before he went limp again.

'Julian? Julian, can you hear me?'

'Reflexive reaction,' explained Chad.

He wiped the blackened wound with the cloth, and placed the bullet within the cloth, careful not to touch it. He passed the cloth back to Rachel who left and returned with bandages and some isopropyl alcohol. She watched as they worked in silence.

When Julian's wound was dressed, Liam stood and turned to Rachel, finally taking in the slightly shorter length of her fiery hair, now falling to her bosom. He offered her a wan smile.

'I'm sorry to barge in on you like this, we had nowhere else to go, not anywhere that would be safe anyway.'

'What the hell is going on, Liam?!' Rachel asked, concern in her voice. She placed her hand on his arm, her eyes darting between his face and clothes.

'I've got something to tell you, and you might not believe me, or maybe it'll scare you, but—'

'Just spit it out, Liam. I've always been on your side for everything. Whatever it is, I'm here for you. Promise.'

Liam met his sister's gaze. 'I'm a vampire.'

Rachel blinked. 'Like, is this a trend you're trying or . . .'

'More like Julian was always a vampire and he turned me when I got shot—'

'Oh my god, you got shot!?'

'And he saved my life.'

'You were gonna die!'

'And now I'm a vampire and the sun melts my insides and silver does that inky snaky thing you saw.'

Rachel mulled that over. Liam had blurted a lot very quickly and he hoped she believed him. She looked at Chad and James – the Sub-Alpha now sat beside Chad.

'Are you *all* vampires?' she asked carefully.

James waved casually. 'I'm a werewolf.'

Rachel scowled. 'I thought werewolves and vampires were mortal enemies.'

'We are,' replied James.

'We don't have to be,' Chad expressed, meeting James's eyes.

James chuckled, taking Chad's hand. 'Then you owe me a kiss, Chad.' Chad smiled back.

'Wait, wait, wait!' Rachel waved her hands about, trying to make sense of it all. 'Let me get this straight, you're, like, actual vampires, for real, for real?'

'Yes,' asserted Liam.

Rachel looked at him and a smile crept on her face. 'Do you have superpowers?'

Liam couldn't help but laugh. 'Sort of.'

'My younger brother's a superhero?' she gasped. 'Can you, like, turn into a bat?' Rachel's eyes were practically bugging out, she looked so excited.

Liam chuckled as Chad let out a loud laugh. 'Oh, how the stories exaggerate our abilities,' the ancient vampire droned.

'No,' confirmed Liam, 'we don't turn into bats, but we do have heightened hearing, among other abilities, such as exceptional speed.'

'Show me your teeth, I want to see your teeth!'

Liam let his canines extend and he bared his fangs at his sister – non-threateningly, of course.

'Aaaaah!' Rachel squealed. 'Oh my god, Liam, you're such a stud, you look so good with those, it suits you!'

'That . . . is *not* the reaction I was expecting,' admitted Chad.

Rachel hugged Liam. 'Thank you for coming out to me – again. I'm so proud of you.' She gave Liam a big slurpy kiss on the cheek.

'I love you too, Rachel.' Relief washed over him and Liam hugged his sister tightly, tears stinging his eyes.

Rachel pulled away and wiped Liam's face. 'He's going to be okay, right?' She looked over at Chad and James who still sat on the bed beside Julian.

Chad nodded. 'Bullet's out. But he needs blood.'

'I've got more liver in the freezer.' Rachel pointed towards the kitchen.

'Human blood.' Liam clarified. They all looked expectantly at Rachel.

'Oh . . . no, oh-no no-no. Me?'

'I wouldn't ask if it wasn't a matter of life and death, Rachel, I promise,' said Liam, his tone earnest. 'Only in the way you're comfortable.'

Rachel thought for a moment. 'I need to shave my legs.'

'Uh, okay?' Chad said, sounding uncertain.

'I mean, I always somehow nick myself when I shave, I'm just that clumsy. So I'll . . . extra nick myself? And you can catch the blood in a bowl or something, yes?'

'That'll work. Thank you!'

Rachel nodded again. 'Okay, let me go get things ready.'

She left the room. Liam let out another relieved sigh. He walked back over to the bed.

'Your sister's hot,' said Chad. 'Voluptuous. She into threesomes?'

Liam slapped Chad's arm. 'Idiot!'

James hissed. 'At least wait until we've shared our first kiss before saying you want to invite a third in this relationship.'

Chad smiled sheepishly and James chuckled. Liam shook his head.

Rachel called Liam into the bathroom and he proceeded as she instructed. It took a few moments, and Rachel yelped at herself, but Liam was able to collect a good ounce of blood into a shooter for Julian without Rachel feeling unwell from some blood loss.

When Liam returned to the bedroom, James and Chad were sitting on the small loveseat, making out, clawing at each other like two lovers wanting to explore every inch of each other's bodies all at once. They reluctantly pulled apart when Liam re-entered the room.

Chad moved to Julian's side and tilted his head up, then Liam poured the blood into his mouth, slowly, allowing Julian to reflexively swallow it. Then they placed his head back down on the pillow. Julian's breathing remained slow and shallow.

Liam sighed. His heart was still racing, and his mind was whirling. It had only been a couple of months since he'd been turned and already there was so much turmoil following them.

Liam gently wiped the side of Julian's mouth with his thumb where a drop of blood remained. He bent down and gently kissed him. As though Julian could sense him, his breathing immediately eased. One deep breath followed another before Julian fell into a normal rhythm as though he were merely sleeping. It gave Liam hope.

Chad eyed Liam with an inscrutable expression before smiling in sympathy. 'Hey,' he said gently, 'he's going to be fine.'

'I just wish things weren't so . . . intense.'

'I promise, some centuries are boring as fuck!' replied Chad.

'By the way, Liam,' began James, 'I'm sorry about some things from the past month. And, well, we don't need to resume our fight from yesterday.'

Liam nodded. 'A lot's happened since then, eh?'

James let out a one-breathed chuckle. 'Yeah. Feels like so much more time has passed.' He looked at Chad. 'I guess I have a thing for vampires. One of them is very good at persuading me to forget another I had my eye on.'

'Glad to hear it,' both Liam and Chad said. The three shared a small laugh. Liam wished Julian was awake to share this moment with them.

Rachel returned to the room. 'Is there anything else you need?'

Liam turned to her. 'You've been great, Rachel, thank you.' She smiled fondly and it warmed Liam's heart – she had always been there, had always supported him, and no words could express Liam's gratitude. Rachel took his hand and squeezed – he didn't need to say more, she knew, she always knew.

'Has it always been just you and your sister?' James asked conversationally.

'As long as we can remember,' replied Rachel.

'No parents?' asked Chad.

Liam and Rachel exchanged a look.

'Our parents disowned him when he announced he was gay in eighth grade,' explained Rachel.

'I'm sorry,' said Chad. 'I forget how in recent centuries people got uptight about these things. When I'm from, it was common knowledge and perfectly acceptable.' He folded his arms, leaning back. 'Of course, the history books won't teach you that. Whatever you want to call me, in my time, there was no need for labels, we merely had lovers, and everyone was entitled to love whomever they wanted. Of course, there came societal challenges, like arranged marriages, power imbalances, lords . . . and slaves and . . . yeah.'

He made one of those faces that said he realised how complex history had actually been throughout all the times he'd lived.

'They didn't disown me,' corrected Liam. 'We chose to leave. *We* cut ties with *them.*'

'They hired a freakin' exorcist!' shouted Rachel. She looked at Chad and James. 'I told them, if they didn't stick their cult in their asses and accept their son as he was, then they would lose both their children.'

Her face contorted in disdain and she shook her head. 'I packed our bags and we left. I was finishing college anyway, so I was able to bribe an aunt, get some money, get a decent job and pay for a house, where we lived together for the longest time. Only this one,' she tussled Liam's hair, 'decided to move out and get his own apartment and leave me high and dry.'

'I didn't leave you high and dry!' protested Liam, suppressing a laugh. 'I found a place a five-minute walk away from where I work!'

'Made you smile though, didn't I?'

Liam realised he was smiling at the fond memories of him and his sister starting a new life together.

Rachel let out a laugh and put a hand to her mouth, blushing.

'What now?' Liam demanded, amused. Rachel shook her head, waving a hand dismissively. 'No, no – go on,' Liam prompted, 'what's going through that mind of yours?'

'Well, your canines were always a bit on the pointy side,' she blurted. 'Now you get to put them to good use.' She winked and burst into laughter, leaning on Liam who merely stared at her, slack-jawed, at once amused and uncertain as to what she was implying.

'My sister, everyone,' he said with a flourish of his hand.

'I'm sorry, uh.' Rachel sighed. 'I'm just . . . You come in here, tell me this crazy story – which I believe by the way – and I give my blood to your boyfriend – sorry fiancé – and then you expect me not to crack jokes? It's a lot to take in.'

'I realise, sorry.'

'It's fine.' She sighed again. 'Anyway, let me know if you need anything.'

'Just some rest,' admitted Liam.

'You can have my bed,' she told Liam. 'You two, no funny business under my roof when I'm in the house.'

'Ooh, you hear that, James, when she leaves the house, we can get up to funny business,' Chad cooed.

'What about you?' Liam asked Rachel.

'I can sit by Julian while you rest,' suggested Rachel.

'What about work?' asked Liam.

Rachel pulled out her phone. A moment later someone answered. 'Yeah, hey,' she began, adding grit to her voice, 'I think I've got this thing in my throat, I need to take some time off.'

Chad and James started whispering flirtatiously to each other.

'Yeah, it's bloody annoying!' Rachel slapped Chad on the arm with the back of her hand. Covering the phone, she mouthed, *Shut up.* 'Yeah,' she said to her boss again, 'I look forward to sinking my teeth into those files once I'm back.'

Liam rolled his eyes. 'I know what you're doing,' he whispered, annoyed, yet he was amused, despite everything.

'Oh, them,' Rachel told her boss, as James reached towards a decorative mantelpiece. She slapped his hand away. 'They keep barking up the wrong tree.' James's eyes widened and he exhaled a laugh as Chad snorted a laugh.

'That's what I was saying!' Liam heard the man on the other side of the receiver exclaim loudly before his voice grew quiet again and he didn't catch the rest of his side of the conversation.

'Yes, yes, of course,' Rachel went on. 'All right, bye now.'

She turned to Chad and James. 'You two, sofas in the living room. Behave. You,' she told Liam, 'bed. I've got this.'

Chad and James left, chuckling. Liam sat down next to Julian. He hated the thought of leaving him, but he was tired and did need rest. He took his hand and brought it to his lips and kissed it.

Suddenly everything that had happened hit him – all the adrenaline left his body, and Liam felt the fatigue overwhelm him. Tears poured down his face again. Rachel was by his side in an instant, wrapping her arms around him.

'Hey, I've got your back, no matter what. I'm here.'

Liam leaned into his older sister's embrace while he wept a bit longer. Then, after a brief comforting chat, he retreated to her bedroom, allowing himself to relax, and sleep took him.

Chapter Eight

Julian regained consciousness cautiously – as he was taught to do. He kept his eyes closed but left just a tiny slit so he could get a sense of his surroundings. He held his breath for a moment as pain shot up his arm, that's when he noted that his wound was bandaged. So someone had dressed it – someone wanted him alive.

A woman sat on a chair near the bed he was in, reading something on her phone. Fiery wavy hair draped over her shoulders. Julian noted that she didn't look alert, which told him his captor probably didn't think he'd regain consciousness this soon.

Without moving, he glanced quickly at her waist. No weapons – his captor's first mistake. He also became aware that he was not bound – his captor's second mistake.

Moving with vampiric speed, he leapt up at the woman, placing his hand on her mouth to silence her. Eyes flaring, he met her gaze as she yelped into his hand.

'You have five seconds to tell me why I shouldn't kill you right here,' he whispered harshly.

Her muffled voice vibrated on his hand and she rolled her eyes. Odd behaviour. Julian released his hold on her mouth but kept her pinned to the wall.

'Say that again?' he demanded.

'I'm Liam's sister.'

Julian froze but did not let go. His eyes widened. 'Rachel?'

'That's me.'

He pressed again. 'How do I know you're telling me the truth?'

She sighed and dropped her shoulders in mild annoyance. 'They brought you in, okay? You're in my house, and . . .' She moved, and Julian tightened his grip on her. She pointed at her leg. 'Lift my pant, you'll see. You drank my blood. So can we just . . . start again? Can you back up maybe? After all, we're going to be in-laws.'

Julian took a moment to take that in. If this woman was a captor, she was awfully good at acting like anything but.

'By the way, did you get him a ring? Liam's a sucker for' – Rachel giggled – 'sorry, but yeah, he's a sucker for those gold bands with engravings on them.'

Julian took a step back. 'I'm sorry.' Julian smoothed Rachel's sleeves, feeling self-conscious. This was hardly the first impression he had wanted to make to his sister-in-law. 'I'm Julian,' he hesitated.

Rachel smiled warmly. 'Nice to finally meet you, Julian. I'm Rachel.'

Julian nodded, still feeling embarrassed. 'So you know?'

'I do now, since this morning.'

'How long have I been out?' inquired Julian, his brows furrowed in thought.

'They brought you in this morning,' Rachel replied. 'Whatever happened to you happened during the night, I think.'

Julian nodded, so not even a full day was he out. He eyed Rachel curiously and a smile curled on the side of his mouth. 'You know, technically, Liam's the one who proposed to me.'

'Oh, he told me it was a mutual proposal.'

Julian thought about it for a quick moment. 'Yeah, actually, it was.' He smiled, thinking of Liam. Rachel's eyes reflected her joy for them. It moved him to know they had her blessing.

'Rachel?' came Liam's voice. 'Are you talking to yourself again? You know it makes you look cra—' Liam stopped in the doorway. 'Julian!'

Before Julian could register what was happening, Liam was in his arms, his lips pressed against his, his kisses sending a fiery rush through Julian's body.

'Sure, pretend I'm not here,' Rachel chided, though she was smiling.

Liam pulled away from Julian, blushing. 'Sorry.'

'I'm just teasing. But the rule stands for the two of you as well, no funny business while I'm in the house. The last thing I want is to hear my brother . . .' She shook her head. 'No offence.'

'None taken,' said Liam. 'I wouldn't want to hear you either.'

Julian felt another wave of pain and winced, feeling suddenly weak. He sat back down on the bed.

'Easy there,' Liam advised. 'That wound did one hell of a number to your arm.'

Julian looked over at his arm. The bandage was a bit bloody. Rachel excused herself and Liam sat on the bed beside Julian.

'We'll be safe here while we lie low,' said Liam. He began undressing the wound – it was still raw-looking, but there was no longer any infection from the silver bullet. Julian noticed Liam's hands were trembling, and though his senses were a little subdued, he could hear Liam's racing heart.

'You're afraid.' Julian took Liam's hands in his.

'I was terrified I'd lose you, Julian,' Liam admitted. His eyes twinkled before Liam blinked back his tears. 'I guess now we both know how it feels.'

Julian kissed Liam tenderly, resting his forehead on his lover's. 'Thank you, for saving me.'

Liam smiled. 'Only what you'd do for me.'

Rachel returned with Chad and James in tow, and a wet cloth and new bandage. 'Right, I'll let you catch up. I'll go prepare something to eat.'

'Allow me,' offered James. 'You've done a lot for us already. Just show me where everything is, I'll cook us a meal.'

'Oh, James, that's so sweet of you, thank you.' She hesitated. 'Do vampires eat?'

Chad chuckled. 'We eat, we drink, we feast, we simply require blood from time to time.'

'And werewolves definitely eat, the rawer the meat the better.'

'Medium-rare for me, thanks,' said Rachel, lifting her chin and giving him a pointed smile.

She and James left the room. Chad swooped in and scooped Julian into a hug. 'Damn, I'm so relieved.' He cleared his throat, stepping away from Julian. The two suppressed smiles.

They had always been friends, though sometimes their friendship had been strained. Recently, Julian had gotten possessive of Liam in front of him, but Chad had not been vexed – Chad had been there since his turning, and Julian was glad he was here with them now.

'No news, then?' asked Julian, as Liam redressed his wound.

'None,' replied Chad.

Julian took a moment to reflect on the events. 'What do we know about what happened? Someone obviously coordinated an attack on both us and the Cromwells. Like we concluded yesterday, someone had to have leaked the information to the cops. There were too many of them and it was way too organised.'

'And they had silver bullets,' completed Chad. 'We can't trust anyone anymore, except for us.'

'And the elders?'

'I trust Stella and Wilbur not to sell us out,' asserted Chad, 'they're ancient – not as ancient as me, but I digress. I also trust Richard, though he went underground before the attack. However, I believe he is innocent, for the attack was too coordinated, it had to have been done by someone who was present. We've been together a long time, the elders and I as a coven, but I wouldn't put it past anyone else, as angry as it makes me.' He pressed his lips in a thin line. 'We have to face facts – we were betrayed, Julian. The vampires and werewolves both.'

'James doesn't know anything about it? You trust him?' Julian asked Liam the question, suspecting Chad and James had already moved past flirting, knowing Chad.

'I trust him,' Liam confirmed.

Julian pulled out his phone and looked at it. 'No texts, no emails, no calls. Then we wait.' He put a hand to his forehead and sighed. 'Fuck!' His eyes stung with tears. He looked at Liam. 'I promise, this is not the life I wanted to drag you into, Liam.'

'I know. But I would rather be alive with you and part of this life than not.'

Julian looked from Liam to Chad, the ancient man's usual jovial expression was replaced with one of sorrow and dread. 'Chad?'

'It's bad, Julian. You saw, all the dead werewolves and vampires scattered across the snow. To have brought enough silver to do all that.'

'Who shot me? Was it more Cromwells?'

'Yes.' Liam tensed. 'Cromwell Junior's henchmen. I killed them. I killed all three of them.'

'Tore them apart, you mean,' muttered Chad.

'Wow,' breathed Julian. Liam really was learning to use his vampiric abilities fast.

From the kitchen, Rachel's shrill laughter carried to the room. 'She took the news all right, then?' asked Julian.

'Oh my god, Julian,' Liam sighed, tilting his head back, 'she keeps making puns.'

'Yeah,' Julian's mouth quirked into a smile, 'she made one earlier – I think it was inadvertent.' He chuckled. 'I like her.'

'And before either of you ask, we can totally trust her,' Liam assured.

'Hey Liam,' began Chad, 'did your parents actually hire an exorcist?'

'Oh, you told him the story?' asked Julian.

'Rachel did – and yes. They were convinced I was possessed by a demon.'

Chad snorted. 'Sorry to break it to you, but now that you're a vampire, according to some legends, you *are* a demon. After all, we are' – he and Julian chanted together – 'supernatural.'

Liam snickered. 'Yeah well, I'd rather people think I'm a demon because I'm a vampire, than think I'm possessed by a demon because I'm gay.'

Chad pointed at him. 'Very true.'

'I remember what they told me when Rachel and I left,' said Liam. As he continued, Rachel's voice from the doorway voiced the same thing at the exact same time in a preachy tone. 'Nothing can save you now!'

'Ugh, give me a break!' Rachel complained. 'Their loss . . . for not loving their son as he was.' She walked over to Liam and brushed some of his long bangs out of his face. 'And my gain for having my brother's love all to myself without having to share him with any other family member.'

'Yeah, I consider myself one of the lucky ones,' mused Julian. 'My folks accepted me as a gay man, and then they accepted me as a vampire.' Rachel and Liam both smiled warmly at Julian's recounting.

'They donated a lot to the coven,' added Chad. 'Funds *and* blood. They were awesome.'

'I think my mom had a crush on you,' laughed Julian. He sighed, smiling fondly. 'They were the best parents I could have asked for. I miss them, but I know they lived long and happy lives, and I know that they were proud of me. I'm glad the coven could offer them a place to be taken care of when they reached that age before they passed away.'

Liam took Julian's hand in his and interlaced their fingers. 'Some of us get to be blessed with supportive family members, even if it's just the one, that one matters a lot.' He smiled up at Rachel. 'And at least I am blessed with the best sister.' Their eyes twinkled as they beamed at each other.

James returned. 'It's cooking, almost ready.'

'Thank you, James.' Sitting on the bed between Liam and Julian, Rachel turned to Chad. 'So tell me Chad, how long *have* you been around?'

'He won't say,' Julian replied in a serious tone, 'but . . . rumour has it,' he leaned towards Rachel, dropping his voice conspiratorially,' 'he's from Atlantis.'

'No way!' Rachel gasped.

Julian grinned. 'I have no idea, I'm just pulling your leg.'

Rachel playfully slapped him. 'You're just as bad as my brother; you two are made for each other!' Everyone laughed.

'And whatever ancient myths exist,' said Chad, 'exist as myths for a reason. I will neither confirm nor deny their existence.'

'So, like, the actual Underworld of Greek mythology?' Rachel asked excitedly. 'Cthulhu?'

Chad put his hands out, shrugging. 'Eh.' He winked at Julian, who shook his head, chuckling.

Rachel turned to look at Liam. 'You know what you boys need, a good night out. You need to act like normal humans, just doing normal human things. So after dinner, you're taking me out to thank me for my awesomeness. I'll get some of Liam's old clothes out so you can change into something more appropriate, just dump all your bloody clothes in the washing machine, and—'

Her phone chimed. She quickly glanced at it and blushed. Julian was acutely aware of her increasing heart rate.

'Rachel?' Liam asked, his voice almost suspicious.

'It's nothing.'

Liam grabbed the phone from her hand and looked at the message. 'Aw, "hope you're feeling better."' Liam read playfully. He grinned boyishly at his sister. 'Who's Keisuke?'

'Someone at work, he's just a friend. Now give that back.'

Liam gaped at Rachel. 'Oh my god, Rachel, you're in love. My sister's in love,' he teased.

'Shut up, Liam, or I'll broadcast to the whole damn world that you're a vampire.'

'Tattle-tale!'

'You realise the two of you are acting like literal five-year-olds right now, right?' joked Chad.

'Give it back, Liam. Don't be such a dick and give me back my phone!'

Liam laughed, texting away.

'What the fuck, Liam!'

'My brother's in town and we're going for a drink after supper if ever you want to join in on the fun.' Liam read aloud. 'And, sent.'

Rachel was so red in the face, Julian was certain she'd combust into flames. He could sense her excitement and anxiety like it was his own.

'Deep breaths, sister,' said Liam.

Rachel slapped his arm, making a face. She pinched the bridge of her nose. Then, shaking her head, she stood and left the room, leaving Liam laughing, still holding her phone.

* * *

The bar they went to was moderately busy, with several groups of people enjoying drinks, some loud, others not. Several patrons were enjoying a game of pool at the back of the bar, while many others sat at the bar itself.

With a set of fresh clothes and having cleaned their jackets as best as they could, the group looked like any ordinary humans going out for some drinks.

Liam sat between Rachel and Julian on one side of the round table, Chad and James sat on the other. These two were holding hands and overtly gazing flirtatiously into each other's eyes.

'So, Rachel,' began Chad.

'Chad?' warned Liam, knowing where this was going.

'You into threesomes?'

Liam rolled his eyes. Rachel blushed and gaped at them.

'Uh, not really, no.' She passed her hand through the back of her hair.

'Not even with . . .' Chad leaned forward and mouthed, 'a vampire and a werewolf.'

'Can you not hit on my sister, Chad, please!'

Chad lifted his hands in surrender, leaning back.

'I second that,' said James. 'Much as I'd love to indulge in a beautiful woman such as you,' James turned his smile from Rachel to Chad, giving him a meaningful stare, 'I'm more of a monogamy type of guy.'

'Noted,' said Chad, looking flustered by the genuine smile on James's face. He tucked a short strand of curly black hair behind his ear, as James caressed his knuckles with his thumb.

'Hey, Rachel,' a tall man dressed far too business-like to fit in at this bar said. He was older than Liam had imagined, then again, his sister *was* thirty-one. And he was very handsome. His shoulder-length black hair was pushed behind his ears, ebony eyes fixed on Rachel, and he wore a business suit under a gentleman's black overcoat.

'Keisuke.' Rachel beamed at him. It was obvious to Liam that Keisuke had feelings for Rachel just by the way he was looking at her.

Liam stood and offered him his hand. 'Hi, I'm Liam, Rachel's brother.'

'Keisuke Matsuoka,' the man replied formally with a quick bow. 'Nice to meet you.' Then Keisuke shook Liam's hand.

Liam motioned the only available chair between Julian and Chad, and Keisuke sat down.

'This is my fiancé, Julian, and our . . . close friends, Chad and James.'

'Nice to meet you all,' said Keisuke. He looked at Liam. 'Rachel's told me so much about you, she's always singing your praises.'

Liam grinned. 'Glad to hear it.'

Keisuke seemed awkward, looking about as he was. He did look out of place in his suit.

'So what do you do, Keisuke?' asked Liam.

'Head of sales,' replied Keisuke. 'Just came from a meeting. Closed another deal. Having minored in diplomacy keeps paying off.'

'He closes every deal,' Rachel said admiringly. Keisuke blushed.

Chad turned to him and said something in Japanese.

Keisuke perked up. 'You speak Japanese?'

'A little bit. I've learnt many languages in . . . over the years,' explained Chad. 'I've travelled a lot and I actually lived in Japan during . . . a time.'

Keisuke relaxed somewhat and the conversation eased. 'What line of work do you do to know so many languages?'

'Oh, I've just been fascinated with travelling and visiting different cultures,' replied Chad.

'Whereabout in Japan have you lived?' asked Keisuke. Chad mentioned several cities and villages. 'The village my parents are from is such a lovely place. I've visited many times.'

'Were you born here or in Japan.'

'Here.' Keisuke looked at Rachel. 'I'm glad my parents decided to immigrate. I've met some amazing people I would otherwise not have known.'

Liam suppressed the urge to nudge his blushing sister. It was becoming more clear that Keisuke felt the same way about her as she did about him.

The conversation about travel continued for a bit before it returned to Rachel and Keisuke working together in sales and accounting. Everyone was chiming in and laughing the more they all got to know each other.

Liam was finally starting to think this whole 'lying low' thing and acting like normal beings might not be so hard after all.

'Hey beautiful!' A drunk man barrelled towards the table, slurring his words and stinking of booze. He leered at Rachel. 'You thirsty? Want to drink me?'

'Excuse me, sir,' began Keisuke, 'but perhaps you can refrain from speaking to the lady in such a crude manner.'

'Pfft, who the hell are you, her boyfriend?' The drunk man eyed them all. 'You *all* her boyfriends?'

'Oh my god, loser! Get lost!' complained Rachel.

'Just ignore him,' said Chad.

The man laughed. 'Can I join your fun, beautiful? You already have all these men, what's one more?' He placed a hand on her shoulder. Both Liam and Keisuke stood at once.

'Get your hands off her!' demanded Keisuke, his tone low and authoritative.

'Oooh, I'm trembling in my boots.' He wavered. 'Fine, have her all to yourselves. Didn't realise there was a maximum number of guys allowed to a gang bang, fat fuckin' slut.'

Liam grabbed the man's arm, squeezing tightly. 'What did you just call my sister?' he seethed.

'Liam, it's fine. He's just a drunk idiot.'

'I suggest you leave,' Liam threatened, 'unless you want me to rip you limb from limb.'

'Pfft!' The man spat in Liam's face. Liam shoved him away – harder than he anticipated – and the man careened right into a group and onto their table, spilling everything on it.

The group cried out in protests and complaints, shoving him off and into another group. The man tried to punch someone who retaliated, shoving the man back towards Liam. The drunk patron tried to punch Liam who punched him instead. He staggered back, tripping on himself, and fell.

Liam sighed, but the damage was done, as all around them, people complained, shoving and punching each other, and the fracas crescendoed.

Someone tried to punch James, missing and falling at his feet.

'You don't want to do that, my friend,' warned James, rolling up his sleeves, exposing his neatly groomed arm hair, and cracking his knuckles.

A fist found Liam's jaw and another drunk patron swung at Chad. Someone bumped into Rachel who staggered back into another woman who spilled her drink all over herself.

'Uah, my top! You bitch!'

Keisuke was by Rachel's side and took the shove from the drunk woman for her. *How gallant,* Liam thought, before he had to duck another punch.

Some guy tried to punch Keisuke, but the man blocked the punch, bringing his arm up. He dropped down into a crouch and swung his leg out to trip his attacker before jumping up and standing protectively in front of Rachel.

Liam was forced to bring his attention back to defending himself, as they all fended off drunk brawlers.

Slowly, the cluster of fighting that had remained in their area of the bar spread throughout the entire bar.

Someone further back shouted out: 'Bar fight!' and threw someone onto the pool table.

Chaos ensued as everyone began fighting everyone, while Liam and his friends were left dodging drunken punches and falling patrons as they scurried out of the bar.

* * *

Rachel sat on a chair in the living room in front of Liam, Julian, Chad and James, looking miffed. The four men sat on the long sofa, looking sheepish under the woman's stern glare.

Keisuke had gone home after having politely expressed that the night had been an interesting one – that was one way of putting it.

'So much for lying low,' Julian muttered.

'Shut up!' Rachel ordered. 'You'll speak when I tell you to.' Julian shut his mouth.

Liam opened his mouth to speak and then closed it again – probably sensing, as Julian did, that it was not the time.

Rachel swept her hair back. 'While I appreciate you defending me, how do you expect me to protect you if you can't act like normal human beings!'

'Because we're not human, are we?' said Chad. Rachel glared at him; he deflated ruefully, casting his eyes to the floor.

'I just wanted a nice night out. And Liam, you *had* to invite Keisuke over, fine, and then a brawl? With the *entire bar*? I'm trying to help you here, I'm trying to get my bearings too. The entire bar . . . in a brawl!'

'Yeah, we messed up big time,' admitted Liam, 'and drew unwanted attention to ourselves. We're sorry. It's just . . .' He sighed. 'You've always been the one to defend me whenever a bigot said anything. This time it was a sleaze calling you names and you didn't deserve that.'

'I get that, and I appreciate you coming to my defence. This isn't my first rodeo with sleaze balls and douchebags trying to get under my skirt,' she bugged her eyes out at Chad, who shrunk further under her gaze, 'but threatening to tear him limb from limb when you actually *can*, and when you know someone out there is trying to kill all the vampires and werewolves!'

Rachel began to laugh, though it sounded more maniacal than anything else. 'God, that sounds . . . I feel like I'm in some sort of weird action movie.' She sighed. 'Look, I'm not mad at you, I'm *worried* about you.'

Rachel's eyes landed on Liam. 'You come here, covered in blood. You tell me you became a vampire because you were gonna *die* otherwise. How do you think that makes me feel? You don't call for weeks while you're lamenting Julian leaving – which, okay fine, turns out was a misunderstanding – and then you come here, tell me you're a vampire, needing my blood for your boyfriend – sorry, fiancé, and that's the other thing you omit to tell me, you're freakin' engaged – and your life is in danger! And I'm supposed to keep it together and act normal and not freak out about any of it?'

'I did find you had taken everything uncharacteristically well initially,' remarked Chad. 'But yeah, it's normal to experience shock when learning about all this.'

He turned to Liam. 'I've seen humans lose consciousness and worse because the truth is too unfathomable – like your boss. I think your sister – who is awesome by the way,' he added quickly, looking at Rachel before turning back to Liam, 'just hit her breaking point of shock. This is where the excitement of it all comes crashing down.'

'Thank you for the understanding, Chad,' said Rachel. 'I just . . . I feel so useless.'

'Rachel,' began Liam, 'I know you've protected me all your life. I may have superpowers now but it doesn't mean I've stopped needing my sister.'

The tears came pouring down her face and Liam stood to take his sister in his arms. Julian realised that in the adrenaline of it all, they had lumped a lot on Rachel, expecting her to take it and be fine with it.

Embarrassed, Rachel pulled away. 'Okay, I'm good now.'

'Should we call Keisuke for him to comfort you?' Liam murmured to Rachel, his voice was filled with caring.

'Shut up!' Rachel mumbled, suppressing a smile. She stood and squeezed Liam's hand before going to bed.

Liam returned to the sofa. 'It's your turn with the guest bedroom,' he told Chad and James. 'We can take turns each night.'

Chad and James left excitedly.

'They are so not going to *not* get into funny business,' Liam muttered. He turned to Julian. 'How's your arm?'

'Some chick landed a good punch right on the wound, but it's otherwise all right,' replied Julian. He chuckled. 'So much for lying low and acting like normal humans, eh.'

He took Liam in his arms as they lay down on the couch. 'We'll manage,' said Liam.

'We always do. We just need to not get into brawls.' They chuckled. 'We need to help your sister however we can while we're here, she's really been awesome so far.' Julian truly felt much gratitude towards his future sister-in-law. 'I hope we hear from Stella and Wilbur soon.'

'You think they're all right?' asked Liam.

'I'm certain they are. They're resourceful,' replied Julian. 'We just need to stay away from any place associated with vampires or werewolves to maintain our cover.'

Liam nodded. They closed their eyes and dozed off to sleep.

Chapter Nine

A little over a week elapsed and there was still no news from neither the coven nor the Sharpe pack. Liam and his crew aided Rachel within the household, seldom venturing beyond its walls, and made sure to maintain a low profile if they did. Rachel returned to work and proceeded as though everything was normal. She simply told folks who asked that her brother and his friends were staying with her while they were in town.

It was the weekend again, and the clouds were thick and dark with accumulating freezing rain, or Liam figured based on the forecast. Rachel was getting ready to go to the shops.

'I'll go with you,' Liam offered.

'Uhm, hello, daylight?' reminded Rachel.

'It's overcast. I should be fine for an hour or so before my skin starts to react and I start to weaken. Plus we'll be *inside* the store. Besides, you've been doing so much – feeding four supernatural men. Let me help.'

'Fine, but if you melt from the inside out, I'm not mopping up your mess.' Rachel grabbed her purse and car keys, heading for the door.

'Love you two, sis,' chuckled Liam.

He followed her to the car. He stood by the car for a minute, assessing, and realised it felt very different from direct sunlight. He nodded, confirming to Rachel, and away they drove.

Rachel had previously purchased some clothes for each of them, seeing as they had escaped with only their battle-worn garb, and even with what Liam had left at the house when he moved out, it wasn't enough. To top it off, James was more muscular than the rest of them and had already ripped three shirts. James had teasingly boasted about his huge biceps.

The two siblings stood in a grocery aisle, already having picked up meat that contained a lot of blood, and some boudin. It would serve its purpose.

Rachel was reading the ingredients to a dessert product when another woman's voice squealed out, 'Keisuke?'

Rachel's head whipped up, looking around. Liam came to stand next to her. 'Don't look so flustered, you see him at work all the time.'

'Yes, but that's different. And we haven't exactly talked about the other night – the brawl. He's so professional at work.' She placed the item in the cart. 'Unlike Chad, he's a perfect gentleman.'

'Oh, come on, you enjoy it when Chad teases you about a threesome.'

'It's flattering, I admit, but I know he only sees me as eye candy. He definitely has a thing for James, though – more than just physically, I mean.'

Rachel started towards the cash, grabbing a box of cereal from a shelf, when Keisuke came into view, talking to a tall and stylish woman who was smiling all too widely. Rachel stopped and stared – Keisuke didn't notice them. Without hesitation, the woman wrapped her arms around Keisuke and kissed him – and Keisuke didn't stop her.

Liam gaped as the kiss elongated. Okay, he had not expected that.

Rachel dropped the cereal box, cursing under her breath. She bent to pick it up as Keisuke abruptly pulled away from the woman, noticing Liam and Rachel for the first time.

'Rachel,' he breathed.

Rachel cleared her throat, ignoring him, hurrying to the checkout.

'Rachel, this isn't what you think.'

'Really?' Liam clapped back. 'You're really going to pull that line?' Rachel scrambled ahead. Liam lowered his voice, hissing his anger as he spoke. 'I saw your tongue twine with hers. Whatever that was, just don't string my sister along. She thought there was something between the two of you – I thought so too. It seems we were mistaken.'

'Please, I swear, it's not—'

Liam thrust up his finger in warning. He walked to the cash register where his sister was already paying the cashier. He helped her take the bags of groceries and stepped outside. Keisuke hurried after them, calling out Rachel's name.

Liam felt a sting on his skin and a pang hit him. He looked up at the sky. 'Shit,' he cursed – the clouds were parting. 'We need to get home now, Rachel.' He pointed up at the sky.

'Oh, don't worry, we're going home immediately.'

'Rachel, wait, I want to explain!' Keisuke called out.

Rachel whirled on him. 'I don't want to hear it, Kei.' Then she spun back around and continued.

Doing his best to look normal, Liam rushed to the car and slumped into the passenger seat, breathing heavily. 'Drive,' he managed, his voice gritty, 'and put your foot on it.'

'Don't worry, I will.'

Rachel drove right past Keisuke who was still trying to protest, racing after them towards the car.

It didn't take long before Liam and Rachel were in the driveway and Liam ran into the house, panting. He clung to the corridor wall, regaining his bearings.

Rachel slammed the door behind them. She threw the bags of groceries on the floor and immediately began pacing.

'Everything all right?' Julian emerged from the kitchen, Chad and James in tow. His eyes widened and he was instantly by Liam's side, propping him up.

'Yeah, I just need a few. But Rachel . . .'

'I'm such an idiot!' Rachel hissed. She threw her arms up in defeat. 'I don't even know what I was thinking! I was convinced he felt the same way. The things he says to me sometimes, the way he looks at me.' She put a hand to her forehead. 'And all this time he was with another woman.'

'We saw Keisuke at the grocery store kissing another woman,' Liam quickly explained.

'How could I think he felt the same way about me as I did about him?!' Rachel went on. She stopped pacing and broke down into tears. 'I'm so stupid, Liam. I'm not even dating him and I feel like he cheated on me. I have *the worst* taste in men!'

Liam walked over to her, already recovered from his stint in the sun, and took her in his arms. She buried her face in his shoulder.

'Do you need ice cream?' Liam asked in comforting tones, stroking her hair. Rachel nodded. 'Rom-com?' Rachel nodded. 'And the rest of us to tell you how much of an idiot Keisuke is?' Rachel nodded.

She lifted her head. 'I'll even let you boys choose the movie.'

Her phone chimed just as Chad had started a wisecrack and Rachel pulled her phone out and stared at it as a stream of text messages came in. 'Keisuke.'

Another message.

Then another.

Her phone began to ring.

Liam peered over and saw the messages.

Rachel, please let me explain.

I want to tell you who that was and what it was about.

Please, Rachel, you mean so much to me.

I don't want to lose you.

'He's certainly texting like someone who was already dating her,' remarked Chad, looking over Liam's shoulder as he and James began towards the living room.

'We weren't, so it's stupid.' Another message came in. Screaming in anger, Rachel threw her phone across the hall. In one swift motion, Julian caught it in mid-flight.

'Come.' Liam steered Rachel towards the living room where Chad and James were already looking over her collection of rom-coms. Julian placed the phone on the table in the kitchen and proceeded to put the food away.

Well, it certainly was a typical day, Liam thought to himself, with ordinary non-life-threatening problems. Liam was glad he could be here for his sister, sitting on the couch, watching a movie he had no particular interest in but that brought a smile to his sister's lips.

Outside, it became overcast again. Freezing rain began to patter and the sun set.

A persistent knock came at the door.

'A hundred bucks says that's him,' muttered Chad, sounding excited.

Liam went to the door and opened it – Chad had been right. Standing out in the freezing cold rain was

Keisuke, his shoulder-length black hair already wet and plastering the sides of his face.

'Liam, is Rachel with you? Please, I need to speak with her.'

Rachel stepped up behind Liam. 'I'm too upset. Go away.'

Liam began to shut the door. Keisuke placed his hand on the door to stop it.

'Please!' he insisted. He was drenched and shivering now, and definitely looked like a character from one of the rom-coms from Rachel's collection. 'I owe you an explanation.'

The others stepped forward. James folded his arms, flexing his large biceps as Chad stared down at Keisuke in condescension. Yet, that did not deter the tall man from taking another step as he steadily stared at Rachel, yearning in his dark eyes.

Rachel turned to leave.

'I'm in love with you, Rachel!'

Rachel froze and slowly turned around – her heart rate increased.

'She's my ex,' Keisuke went on. 'Look, I should have told you about her. I was . . . with her for a long time and the break-up tore me up inside. For a long time, I still loved her. I was scared to be with someone else, someone new, to start all over again. And for a long time, I delayed telling you how I felt. But as time went on, it became increasingly clear that I was falling in love with you.'

'Then why did you kiss your ex?' demanded Rachel.

'I wasn't expecting her to be in town,' explained Keisuke. 'But when I saw her, I wanted to make sure – needed to be sure – that I was over her before I committed to another woman. So I let her kiss me and I kissed her back to see if I felt anything like I did before.'

Rachel crossed her arms. Keisuke took a step into the house, anxiety and determination on his face; Liam could sense his heart racing.

'I felt nothing for her. It's all gone,' declared Keisuke. 'Everything I ever felt for her has left me. And so now I know for sure; I am ready to be with you, to let you in, if you'll let me.' Chagrin reflected in his eyes. 'I'm sorry you had to see that, I'm sorry I hurt you. I've been trying to build up the courage to tell you how I feel, to take that leap again to be with someone else, except now I fear I've lost you before I could even show you what it means to be loved by me.'

Rachel stared at Keisuke for a moment.

Liam glanced at the others and they each gave a subtle nod – they knew how this story was going to end.

'I'm in love with you, Rachel,' Keisuke declared again. 'And I'll do everything to show it to you.'

Liam and the others slowly retreated, grabbing their coats and heading for the door at the back of the house. Before they reached it, the front door had slammed and Rachel's arms were wrapped around Keisuke, who pressed her against the wall as the two hungrily devoured each other's mouths. The passion in Keisuke's creased brows and the way he held Rachel told Liam how much he loved and desired her.

He smiled, seeing his sister's joy as she smiled at Keisuke between heavy kisses. Then both made a sound that indicated that Liam should have already vacated the house.

Liam urged the others quickly out the back door. 'Yup, yup, heading out,' they said.

Shivering, they took a few steps forward. 'So . . . we give them . . . what, a couple of hours should do?' asked Chad.

'I've got her car keys,' said Liam, dangling the keys in front of his face.

'Fantastic!' Chad whooped.

They made their way around the house to the car and hopped in; Liam in the driver's seat, Julian in the passenger seat, and Chad and James in the back.

Chad let out a loud sigh of relief as Liam turned the heating on in the car.

'What now? We're not going to just sit here like creeps, waiting for them to be done reconciling,' said Julian.

'Reconciling and starting their new relationship,' corrected Liam.

'We could stake out some of the safe houses,' suggested James, 'from afar, I mean, see if anyone's there. We might not know if anyone's been, but it's worth a quick drive.'

'Is that safe, though?' objected Chad. 'We're supposed to be lying low, remember?'

'Then what else do you suggest?' growled James. 'It's frustrating, not knowing what's happened to the rest of my pack?'

'And you think it isn't angering for me not to know what's happened to the rest of my coven?' retorted Chad. 'I've known some of them for centuries. They're my brothers and sisters, mothers and fathers . . . former lovers. You think I'm not plagued by what happened, you think I'm not scared to know what's come of them? You think I don't like not knowing who sold us out? That we can't trust anyone aside from the four of us!'

'Hey, hey, guys!' Julian spoke loudly. 'You're not angry at each other, so stop acting like you are.'

'I'm sorry,' said James, his voice low and regretful.

'Werewolves aren't the only ones whose kin mean everything to them,' Chad pointed out. 'We've got our covens – and even members from the other covens, we're close with them. There is a mutual sense of family with many of us. Sure, some decide they want to harm humans and don't care about the rules we've been abiding by for centuries – the rules that some of us have pushed for since millennia ago – and they are a problem, but they're not the ones who landed us in this mess.'

'Something doesn't add up, though,' voiced Liam.

'No, and until we hear from the others, it might not,' said Julian. 'We just need to stick together and we'll be fine.' He leaned back in his seat.

'So we're really just going to sit here and look like creeps?' asked Liam.

'Nope!' Chad pulled out a joint from his coat.

'Since when do you have a joint on you?' asked Liam, turning even more to look at Chad in the passenger side backseat.

'During the brawl, some dude had a whole case of them in a box fancy enough to rival Stella's snuff box.' Chad pulled out the bronze box and waved it about. 'I was a pickpocket once, and now we're four men respecting our host's no-smoking policy, about to enjoy a doobie.'

Liam laughed and Julian snorted, grinning. 'I hope you have a lighter to go with that, at least, or we look like idiots.'

Chad waved the lighter.

'Well, hello my hippie days,' cheered Julian.

Chad lit the joint up and took a nice long puff, smoking out circles like a pro. They passed the joint around, giggling like teenagers at all their own stupid jokes and enjoying the mellowness of it all as a nice buzz washed over Liam.

James inhaled a last drag of the joint. It lit up red and he rolled down the window, blowing out the smoke as he flicked the butt out. He rolled the window up again, letting out a guttural sigh, his lips curling into a satisfied smile.

'Hey Julian,' began Chad, as he pulled out another joint, his expression and tone completely grave all of a sudden. Julian turned more to look at Chad. 'Do you think Zack and Zanitha got out all right?' He bowed his head. 'I mean, they've been presumed dead before – so many times, I've lost count. They always got out unscathed, or almost.'

'They're resourceful,' Julian reassured, 'I'm sure they got out of there in time.'

'They weren't at the estate we hit,' muttered Chad.

'You heard what Stella said at the club,' said Julian. 'They'll have gone underground to lie low.'

'You heard that?' Chad's eyebrow quirked up. 'Thought you two were too busy getting it on to notice anything around you.' Chad tried to smile before nervously chewing his lip.

A sedated silence followed.

'Chad and the twins once dated,' Julian explained gently.

'Both of them!?' exclaimed Liam.

'Not at the same time,' retorted Chad, 'and that was over a hundred years ago already.' He chuckled. 'And then there's Mandy.'

'Wait, you dated her too?!' exclaimed Liam.

'No, Mandy's like my sister.' Chad smiled fondly. 'I trained her, and I've always looked out for her. She was fighting next to me at the manor until we went in separate directions. I hope she got out of there alive too.'

There was a brief pause. 'What happened between you and the twins, though?' asked James. 'A hundred years isn't that long for a vampire your age. You aren't dating either of them now, so . . .'

'Things . . . changed,' replied Chad, '*we* changed, but we continued to care about each other. Sometimes it's just time to move on, you know, it's just . . .' His voice became solemn again. 'I never stop loving someone once I fall for them. And when you've been around as long as *I* have,' he paused briefly, a sombre melancholy twinkling in his eyes, 'it hurts when you lose someone you love, even if you're no longer with them.' He whispered, 'It hurts so much.'

'Is that why you're such a flirt who doesn't commit?' James asked softly.

'It's easier to bounce from one-night stand to the next than to lose someone you care so deeply for,' replied Chad.

'But isn't it worth it to share happiness with that person, even if it's temporary?' James gently caressed Chad's cheek with the back of his hand.

Chad looked at James. 'Look, you need to know that, when you're with me, like, *really* with me, I fall fast and hard, and there are a lot of intense emotions.'

Liam and Julian smiled affectionately at each other, understanding the very intense emotions he meant. The three vampires exchanged a gentle smile in understanding.

James conveyed his tenderness to Chad, his hand still caressing his face. 'Well, it so happens that I'm the same way.' He shot Liam a glance before returning his gaze to Chad. 'And sometimes one crush leads to one worth investing real emotions in.'

Chad lifted his eyes and looked at James with longing in his eyes. 'Let's just . . . let's just keep things casual for now and see where that leads us, yeah.'

'I can work with that,' replied James.

Chad nodded, then he sighed, leaning back. Resolve returned to his face. 'All right, no more doom and gloom; we're supposed to be getting high!'

He put the joint to his lips, lighting it up and inhaling deeply. He blew out another elaborate set of circles before passing it to Julian. Thus the group resumed their smoking session, passing around and indulging in a total of three hefty blunts.

When they went back into the house, they were all baked real good, trying to be quiet despite their silly giggling, and tripping over each other. None of them made it to the bedroom, they all flumped into the couches in the living room and fell fast asleep.

<u>CHAPTER TEN</u>

Julian awoke to the smell of bacon and his stomach gurgled. Liam next to him stirred awake. Chad let out a loud snore, bouncing awake. James was already stretching and yawning.

'Slept well, boys?' asked Rachel, eyeing them with curiosity.

'Fabulous,' replied Chad, sounding still a bit buzzed.

'You?' asked Liam.

Rachel blushed and bit her lower lip.

'How many strips of bacon do you want?' Keisuke called out from the kitchen.

All at once, the four men bounced to their feet and hurried to the kitchen where a shirtless Keisuke was cooking breakfast. Liam smiled as Chad raised his brows lasciviously.

Keisuke stopped when he noticed them ogling. 'Oh, shoot. Uh, I should go finish getting dressed.'

'No, no,' interjected Chad, tracing the man's outline in the air with his hands. 'By all means, stay like that. In fact, I think you're overdressed.'

Rachel slapped his arm. 'Idiot!'

'Why does everyone always slap me like that!'

James chuckled. 'If you have to ask . . .' He left the sentence unfinished.

Keisuke put the pan down and closed the stove. He excused himself quickly, looking embarrassed, and when he returned, he had a shirt on. He walked over to the window, reaching for the Venetian blind's pull cord.

'No!' shouted Liam, darting to stop the man, slapping a hand on the cord; Keisuke paused. 'I've got . . . sun sensitivity . . . for my eyes' He hesitated. 'Artificial bright lights are fine but . . . something to do with U.V. and, uh, sensitive retinas.'

'Right.' Keisuke nodded, looking confused. 'I'm sorry, medical terms are not my field of expertise.' He stepped away from the occluded window and began serving breakfast for everyone.

'Sausage seems a bit overcooked,' muttered James.

'Everything's overcooked to you, James,' remarked Chad.

They sat down. Keisuke glanced at his phone.

'No work-related activity at the table,' reminded Rachel. 'It's our day off.'

'Sorry, it's the news that caught my attention. A huge fire early this morning right as the sun was rising.'

Rachel peered over. The other guys were whispering to each other, disinterested in the news. Julian, however, was curious.

'Oh my god,' gasped Rachel. 'That's a . . . huge estate.'

Something in Julian's body told him it was Headquarters and a lump formed in his throat. 'Pass it here?' Keisuke handed him the phone.

The others grew quiet around him as Julian grew tense and let out a slow trembling breath. His jaw tight, he swallowed hard. He read aloud, his voice terse. '"Centuries-old manor goes up in flames early this morning, forcing its occupants to rush out."'

'Fuck,' breathed Chad, peering over Julian's shoulder.

Julian went on. '"Many were stranded within the manor as the flames quickly spread. Some were found . . . dead." Shit.' While vampires could sustain fire, the humans who lived with them could not, and if the manor was burning down, even if the fire was extinguished, the vampires would be forced to scramble; retreating to the basement would make them sitting ducks. The implications of the headquarters being rendered unsafe were dire. '"Officials suspect arson."'

'Of course, it's arson,' growled Chad. 'A fire like that doesn't spread that quickly that fast.'

Julian then realised. 'Someone from *inside the manor* must have set this up. Security to the grounds is so tight.'

'The mole,' said James.

'What's going on?' Keisuke asked warily.

'Wait, is that . . . ?' began Rachel.

'Yeah,' said Julian. 'And look outside. Forcing us out in broad daylight, knowing we won't survive.'

'Come again?' blurted Keisuke.

'Or forcing us to be sitting ducks, and whoever did this knows we'd choose sun exposure to—'

Outside, several car doors slammed shut and Julian recognised the familiar sound of gun hammers cocking in unison.

Liam must've realised the same thing. 'Everybody get down!'

Liam pulled Rachel down with him. Julian grabbed Keisuke and pulled him down, lunging towards the far side of the kitchen, as gunfire erupted and bullets shot through the walls and into the house.

Rachel screamed, covering her face with her hands.

Keisuke spat a curse in Japanese. Then, 'What in heaven's name is happening?' he demanded.

Julian looked over at a bullet on the floor as the gunshots stopped. 'Silver.'

'We're trapped. We're surrounded,' hissed Chad. 'How the hell did they find us?'

'Shit!' growled James.

'We've nowhere to escape to!' Liam sputtered.

'The attic!' said Rachel. 'Go up to the attic.'

'What about you?' demanded Liam.

'I'll deal with whoever that is,' said Rachel, her expression stoic.

'But you don't know how to fight!' protested Liam.

'Maybe, but silver won't kill me. Now go.'

Julian followed Liam to a broom closet where Liam pushed a hatch and leapt up into the attic. Julian, Chad and James quickly followed suit, with James shutting the closet door before joining the vampires. Then they closed up the hatch and moved along the floorboards to an area with an air vent where they could peer into the hallway and living room.

'What's going on, Rachel?' Keisuke wrapped his arms protectively around her. 'Why are your brother and his friends being attacked in your home?'

'It's a long story and I'm sorry I couldn't tell you before now but—'

The door burst open as Cromwell cronies stormed into the house, guns raised. Rachel screamed, again bringing her hands to cover her face.

'Whatever you want, just don't kill me!'

'Who are you?' demanded the leader of that group.

'I'm an accountant, I live here.'

The mobster looked at Keisuke.

'Uh, Head of the Sales department, her boyfriend.' He stepped protectively in front of Rachel to shield her. 'Lay a hand on her and you're dead.'

The Cromwell enforcer laughed, it began as an exhale, then a chuckle, then a raucous laugh. 'You're funny.' He pulled out a knife – it gleamed silver – Keisuke did not flinch or cower. Grabbing and pulling on Keisuke's hand, he slashed the man's palm before the other could react to what was being done to him. It wasn't a deep cut but enough to ensure the silver would enter a supernatural being's blood.

Keisuke screamed out in pain, bringing his other hand to press on the slash as blood surfaced on his hand. The lackeys' leader watched as Keisuke's gash bled onto the rug.

'Huh, interesting.' He took hold of Keisuke's hand, observing it, then let it fall. 'Your turn.' With a slight tilt of his head, he motioned towards Rachel, a sneer curling on his lips.

Julian suspected Rachel knew what they were doing but faked it as well as she could. The man cut her hand open and watched as nothing happened except for blood to seep out.

'Where are they?' demanded the mobster.

'Where's who?' quavered Rachel.

'You know who!'

'It's just the two of us here,' insisted Keisuke. 'Look, whatever you think is here, you've got the wrong house.'

The leader looked at his cronies. 'You think the Intel was falsified?'

The crony shrugged. 'Came from one of the vamps.'

Julian cursed under his breath. So it confirmed it – it was a vampire who sold them out. Up until now, while it became clear early on it wasn't a werewolf, it still could have been one of the humans who allied with them, but no, it was one of their own, and that stung even more.

Julian saw Chad tense beside him and James shake his head. Liam merely stared down at his sister, worry on his face. Julian reached over and took his lover's hand, squeezing gently to reassure him.

Rachel remained unmoving, her breathing a little shaky, but never backing down from her stance. Keisuke had a puzzled expression upon his face, all while he fumed in disdain.

'Okay,' the enforcer said to Rachel and Keisuke, 'but you better be telling the truth, else things'll go real bad for you – and worse for your friends if they're your friends.' He flashed the silver knife and grinned.

They turned heel and left, slamming the door behind them.

'What . . . the fuck!' cried Keisuke. He stared at the shut door, forgetting about the dripping cut on his hand.

The cars drove off, tires screeching. The four hideaways waited until the sounds faded into the distance before they jumped down from the trap in the ceiling above the closet and returned to Rachel and Keisuke. Rachel had already gone to get wet cloths to wipe the blood from her and Keisuke's hands.

'Shit, shit, shit!' cursed Chad as they joined the humans. 'So it really is one of our people who betrayed us.'

'I told you my pack had nothing to do with it, we would never betray our kind,' growled James. 'Something you vamps should learn.'

'Everyone just shut up!' Everyone grew quiet and turned to Keisuke. He wrapped the cloth around his hand and looked up at the others sternly. He let out a shaking breath. 'Can someone please tell me what on earth is going on, why I got shot at, and why some lunatic with a knife cut my hand open?'

Rachel looked apologetic. 'I'm so sorry, Kei, it wasn't safe to tell anyone, and I guess now you're involved. We didn't want to drag you into this.'

'Drag me into what?' Keisuke's voice was tense but his face betrayed concern as he looked from Rachel to the others.

Liam shot Julian and the others a knowing look. 'Let's just show him.'

At once, their eyes flared and their top canines extended to fangs. Keisuke doubled back a step, staring at them. He looked at James who flashed him his claws with a curling wave of his fingers.

'We're vampires,' said Liam.

'And a werewolf,' said James.

They took a beat to let that sink in. Keisuke nodded slowly. 'Legends and myths do come from truth,' he mused. 'All cultures have their versions of supernatural beings. Never thought . . . Okay.' he looked at his hand.

'They cut you with a silver knife,' explained Julian. 'That manor in the article . . . was our headquarters, and a vampire betrayed us to the Cromwells, a crime syndicate that's trying to take over the city, one who knows of our existence and is trying to exterminate us.'

'Should we call the cops?' Keisuke asked carefully, digesting the information.

'No!' everyone else cried out.

'Cops are in on it too,' explained Liam. 'They want to expose us and kill us.'

'Some of them already have,' Chad said under his breath.

Keisuke looked at Rachel.

'I just found out a couple of weeks ago,' she said. She downcast her eyes. 'Listen, Kei, I'm sor—'

Keisuke cupped her face with his hands. 'Whatever danger you face, you shan't face it alone. I meant it when I said I'd show you what it meant to be loved by me.'

Liam's heart leapt for his sister. Keisuke was one hell of a keeper.

'That means that whatever weird reality I'm living now,' Keisuke went on, 'I'm not leaving your side.' Rachel smiled at Keisuke, whose dark eyes bore into hers. 'I love you, Rachel. Nothing will change that.'

'Aw.'

'Chad, shut up,' whispered Liam. 'Rachel . . . It's no longer safe for any of us to stay here.'

Keisuke cleared his throat, looking self-conscious. He turned to the others, interlacing Rachel's hand in his. 'How did they find you here?'

'Must've looked my family up,' Liam figured. 'Or whoever sold us out told them about the meeting at my apartment, and they found the address there.'

'Or followed us and found us,' added Julian. 'Does it matter? We've got a mole in the vampires, who knows us and our history. Whoever the traitor is will have known all the possible places to search for us.'

'They don't know me,' asserted Keisuke, that sexy determined look returning to his face. 'I've got a family cabin up north. Unless someone follows us, they won't find us there.'

Liam nodded.

'Pack up,' instructed Julian. 'We won't be back for a while.'

While packing, they explained to Keisuke all about sun exposure and what it did. So they placed pillows to 'legally' cover the windows in the car and dim the lighting in the car as much as possible.

'They won't be expecting us to leave right away,' explained Julian. 'If they want to tail us, they won't have someone sitting in broad daylight to do it. When they come back tonight and find us gone, it'll throw them off.'

Once they had set everything up so that the vampires were as safe as possible from the sun inside the car, which was fairly roomy, they draped blankets over themselves and over their heads like hoods, and that took care of blocking the rest of the daylight. James sat up front, being the biggest of them. Keisuke drove, while Rachel crammed in the back with the vampires.

She coughed upon entering. 'You really did bake last night, didn't you?'

Chad had many-a-time been the hidden guy in the back of a car at the feet of the other passengers, so that's where he placed himself. They each took turns, rotating the position, since it kept them hidden from the sun best.

While the drive was long, they remained sheltered the whole day through.

It was the middle of the night when they finally reached Keisuke's cabin. They got their things out of the car and efficiently set up the necessary for the vampires to feed.

* * *

When everyone had selected rooms and settled, Liam stepped out for some fresh air. Julian joined him. They walked for a while deeper into the woods.

'Nice, quiet night, isn't it?' observed Liam.

'Much like the ones where we'd stand outside the club,' replied Julian.

Liam looked down and took Julian's hand, inter-lacing his fingers with his. The sensation sent a warmth through Julian's entire body. Liam's touch always did.

'Those plans, when we made them, places we'd visit, where we'd live together . . .' Liam hesitated.

'Hey,' Julian brushed his other hand over Liam's face, gently caressing his cheek with the back of his fingers. 'We can still visit those places and have that house. It'll just be a bit different this time.' Julian bowed his head. 'I'm sorry if for part of those plans . . . if I was dishonest.'

It was Liam's turn to brush his fingers on Julian's face. 'I understand why you couldn't tell me about being a vampire.'

'I never lied about loving you, you know that, right?'

'I know. And now, well, we can make better plans, and start planning out our wedding.' Liam smiled in his handsome way; Julian couldn't help but grin. 'Once things settle down,' he added.

'Yeah, crazy, huh?' Julian sighed. 'But in this remote lodge here in the mountains, I feel we'll be safe. Your sister and her new man really pulled through for us. They're solid, as far as I'm concerned.'

'Yeah, they are. And, well, Chad and James are all right roommates too.' Both men chuckled.

Julian gazed into Liam's eyes, their green hue so vivid in the winter night. 'We've barely had a moment to ourselves lately, we've always snuck about or had to be so quiet.'

Liam's eyes flashed and Julian felt his arousal instantly. Letting out a guttural roar, Julian pushed Liam against a tree, holding his hands above his head, and kissed him feverishly.

Liam chuckled, making his lips vibrate. Julian pulled away. 'You enjoy doing that, don't you?' the blond man teased. 'Pinning me like this?'

'Don't you?'

In response, Liam's lips lunged for Julian's, his tongue gliding along his lips as the two vampire's mouths smacked together once more.

The heat rose in Julian's body, feeling Liam's tongue on his canines. Julian pressed his hand on Liam's face and trailed it down his neck. He stopped at the coat, pulling on the collar to keep Liam from moving away – not that he could go anywhere if he tried. Julian chuckled at the thought.

Liam groaned into Julian's mouth, eliciting a shiver of arousal within him. Julian reached for Liam's belt, undoing it quickly and unbuttoning his pants. His fingers wrapped around his lover's hard length and Liam sighed gutturally.

Julian was still gripping Liam's palms with one hand, keeping his fiancé pinned against the tree. Liam moaned, pulsing his pelvis as Julian began to stroke him.

'Julian,' Liam voiced in a husky tone. 'I want to feel you against me.'

Julian let go of Liam's erection to undo his pants and pull out his own length. Taking both cocks in his hand, he stroked them together.

'Oh, fuck!' Julian whispered. Liam's cock pulsed and both shafts rubbed against each other. The tickle made Julian's pelvis vibrate and he began to slide up and down as he continued to stroke both their cocks.

Liam tilted his head back against the tree, his fingers desperately struggling to break free from Julian's grasp. Julian relented and Liam's hands flew free. He grabbed Julian's coat and began to unzip it. Liam reached under Julian's shirt.

'Uah!' Julian gasped as Liam's cold hands pressed on his skin. The sensation was welcome.

Liam nibbled Julian's lip and more heat rose to his face. Julian let go of their erections as he and Liam tugged at each other's coats, pulling them off.

'This is so fucking hot, Julian. I want to fucking come in the snow!'

Just hearing Liam's declaration nearly sent Julian over the edge. Their cocks continued to rub against each other while the two men undressed. Pulling their shirts over their heads and letting them fall onto the snow, both men wrapped their arms around each other, feeling the warmth of each other's chests against the cold wind that blew.

They let their pants slide down to their feet. Liam squeezed Julian's ass and Julian went back to stroking their cocks. Their lips met again with moans and groans. It was Liam's turn to slide up and down while continuing to hold onto Julian's ass.

Feeling his pelvis throb his elation, Julian cried out. 'Oh, fuck! Yes!'

Both cocks stiffened and Liam shouted as both of them came onto each other's erections, making each stroke more slippery than the last, and ascending Julian's orgasm. Liam leaned back, still holding onto Julian and Julian bucked back and forth as their semen spilled onto his hands and sprayed onto the snow.

Liam lunged forward, grabbing Julian's face in his hands, and kissed him voraciously. Julian lost his balance and the two toppled over into the snow. Julian yelped, then laughed.

'Damn that's cold, but . . .' He was still aroused. 'Fuck, it's also hot.'

Liam began to slide himself up and down, rubbing all the semen onto both their stomachs and chests.

'Oh, fuck, Liam, you're going to make me come again!'

'Yeah? You want that?'

Liam grabbed their erections, stroking vigorously. He came again first, shouting and spewing onto Julian's pelvis. Then he bent and took Julian in his mouth, sucking both of their spills as he sucked his cock.

'Fuck, that's good!'

The snow beneath Julian was cold, his body was hot, and his pelvis was vibrating. He slammed his hands down onto the snow, tilting his head back and screaming as he came into Liam's mouth, feeling everything spin in the night.

With a side smile, Liam slowly slid Julian's cock out of his mouth and came up and kissed Julian, semen still on his mouth and Julian drank it up, licking Liam's lips as both continued to moan as they completed their orgasms.

Liam let himself rest on Julian before Julian urged him up. 'Body's cooling, now I'm really cold for real.'

Liam laughed and stood, offering his hand to help Julian up. Their pants were still at their feet, a bit damp now and cold. Julian pulled Liam's warm body to his and kissed him, feeling every inch of his skin as they devoured each other's mouths before a cold gust of wind made both of them shiver.

Chuckling, they pulled their pants up and dressed again.

'Fuck, that's cold,' Liam laughed. 'But you're right, that was hot.'

Julian bit his lower lip. 'Making love to you is always hot, Liam.'

Liam smiled, kissing Julian, tenderly this time. 'That's because I'm always hot for you, Julian.'

'Look whose turn it is to be corny,' chuckled Julian.

'I guess that makes us made for each other.'

Julian stared into Liam's beautiful green eyes. 'You know, a few months ago, the thought of you being here with me, as a vampire . . . it's a dream come true. I always knew I wanted to tell you what I truly was, but that you're one too now. Since the very moment I met you I felt something for you – I knew I loved you before I knew it was love, Liam.'

'I felt the same way, Julian. I saw your eyes and my heart skipped a beat. It was so intense, I couldn't explain it. I love you, Julian. I always have.'

'Since the moment I first met you,' they both whispered.

'And you're my fiancé.' Julian grinned, unzipping his coat pocket and reaching into it. 'That reminds me.' He pulled out a small jewellery box.'

'Julian,' breathed Liam. 'You shouldn't have.'

'While we were at your sister's, when you were helping her with the broken vase, I snuck out after dusk before stores closed and went to a shop to get you this.' He opened the box where two flat golden rings sat. 'I was told you were a sucker for gold bands.'

Liam's lips were on Julian's and Julian felt Liam's warm tears on his face. He pulled away.

'There are engravings on them.' Julian took one of the rings out. *My love for you is eternal.* He read it aloud. Julian grinned. 'I considered having them say "Your sucker for life," but I thought this would be best.'

Liam laughed. 'That would have been too funny, but I like this.' His eyes twinkled. 'My love for you *is* eternal, Julian.'

'As mine is for you, Liam. Vampires are eternal, so when I say I plan on spending the rest of my life with you, that is for all eternity. That's why . . .' He showed Liam the other ring. This one read, *Eternally yours.* 'This one's yours, as I am yours, for all eternity.'

'They're perfect, Julian.'

The two vampire lovers smiled and kissed again, wrapping their arms around each other. Then they put their rings on each other's fingers.

'So are these our engagement rings?'

'They're our forever rings. Engagement and wedding bands. I just . . . I wanted us to wear them now. Make it more official.'

'I love them,' said Liam. 'I love you.'

After another embrace and a few more minutes of making out, Julian and Liam made their way back into the cabin, where they heard muffled voices arguing – Rachel and Keisuke. Liam put an arm out to stop Julian, craning his neck to listen as both vampires used their abilities to hear the lowered voices as though they were right next to them.

Julian glanced at Liam, who looked worried.

'Just hear me out, Rachel.'

'For the hundredth time, Kei, aliens don't exist.'

Liam quickly put a hand to his mouth and chuckled into it, as Julian snorted in his throat.

'They could be watching humanity right now and we wouldn't even know it. They could be walking among us, disguised, and we wouldn't know it.'

'Kei, we're going around in circles.' Rachel sounded exasperated.

'Rachel, listen, *listen:* vampires exist, werewolves exist, therefore aliens must also exist.'

Liam exhaled a whispered laugh.

'He's got a point, though,' admitted Julian.

As Keisuke proceeded to list his so-called evidence as to why aliens existed, Julian and Liam headed to bed, nuzzling into each other, with Julian holding Liam close to his body.

Chapter Eleven

Their stay at the lodge was deceptively uneventful, yet the absence of any pursuers left them both relieved and unnerved.

Rachel and Keisuke took care of errands during the day, insisting that, even at night, the vampires and James should remain close to the cabin, their presence hidden and far from prying eyes. Rachel was adamant that she do her part in protecting her brother from whatever dangers he might now face.

The two mortals had called work to give notice of prolonged absence – family emergency, they had said, which Liam had to admit, was pretty much the case. Their boss had asked them if they had finally started dating. Apparently, the older man had been waiting for them to get together. The company had no policy against it and the employer was ecstatic to hear Keisuke was accompanying Rachel to help with her family crisis.

Liam fervently expressed his gratitude to his sister. It wasn't every day one showed up unannounced, revealed themselves to be a vampire, only for everyone to get shot at and be led into a harrowing escape from relentless mobsters determined to exterminate their kind. It evoked memories of the times his sister went to bat for him during their youth.

'I'll always have your back.' They had echoed to each other, and they pinky swore. Liam being a vampire now didn't change that promise.

When Feral Night came around, James had ensured to remain close to the cabin, though he'd been self-conscious about the vampires seeing him feral, and none of them ventured out in order to respect his privacy.

After the first week, Rachel and Keisuke hunkered down in the lodge, tackling their work assignments from their laptops. Time stretched on, the weeks blending together in a haze of constant vigilance and ever-pressing dread.

'Triple eights,' gloated James, looking smug as he placed his cards on top of Keisuke's. They all sat around the table, their troubling circumstances momentarily set aside as they enjoyed a card game.

'Triple nines,' declared Rachel, matching his tone.

'Pass,' Julian sighed, disinterested.

'Oooh, triple Aces!' Liam threw his cards down.

Chad grinned. He suavely placed two twos on top of the pile before sweeping it up and casting the cards aside. He placed five sixes.

'Five!' cried Julian, eyes bugging out as he leaned forward in his seat.

Then came the Joker, then a single Two. Chad clapped his hands together, then snapped his fingers and shot a fist into the air. 'And the Asshole becomes the President!'

Liam chuckled, shaking his head.

Two phones vibrated at the same time. Julian fumbled for his phone and stared down at it as Chad did with his. Both men froze, glancing up. The mood in the room quickly shifted.

Liam looked over Julian's shoulder. There was a text message from Wilur. *'Who are you with?'* it read.

'It's Stella,' said Chad.

'Wilbur,' said Julian.

Julian typed a quick reply, letting Wilbur know Liam, Chad and James were with him. Chad did the same, letting Stella know who he was with. Both Wilbur and Stella replied they were together. The coven leaders then called to confirm verbally that their fellow vampires were safe and indeed the ones replying. Then they sent the address of a remote safehouse location.

Immediately, Rachel started barking orders to get everything gathered and organised, instructing Keisuke to pack their laptops while she'd pack their clothes.

'Wait, you're coming with us?' asked Liam.

'Liam, whatever else you are, you're my brother. I'm the one who's going to be walking you down the aisle – you bet your ass I'm following you to wherever this place is. I know I'm just' – she mimicked Chad's mockingly sophisticated accent, – 'a mere mortal,' she smiled, speaking normally again, 'but I'm your sister. I'm sure there are things Keisuke and I can do to help.'

'You're the best, you know that?' Liam hugged her tightly. 'Come on, then – no time to waste.'

From where they were, the safehouse wasn't very far, just a few hours out. It was another cabin in the mountains, just not the same mountains.

As Rachel and Keisuke collected their things upon arrival, the three vampires and one werewolf strode up the path and entered the homey place. In a sitting room just beyond the foyer, with a table in the centre, stood Stella and Wilbur.

'Thank you for coming so promptly,' said Stella.

'Well, we weren't all that far,' Chad stammered, 'though I was hoping we wouldn't be the only ones.' He paused to take a breath. He looked from Wilbur to Stella. '*Are* we expecting anyone else?'

'We didn't know if we could trust anyone else,' replied Stella. 'It took us a while to find a safehouse only Wilbur and I knew and to ensure we were the only ones who had ever used it.'

'We escaped together,' Wilbur interjected.

'We waited for good measure as we gathered some Intel that could help us in our coming war against extermination,' explained Stella. 'We knew whoever betrayed us couldn't be Liam, for he hasn't been a vampire long enough,' she nodded once at Liam, 'and we knew we could trust Julian.' The two nodded to each other in acknowledgement before Stella turned back to Chad. 'We also knew we could trust you.'

'How do you know you can, though?' insisted Chad. His tone betrayed a wavering uncertainty to trust who he'd always known he *could* trust.

'Whoever betrayed us wasn't a werewolf, that much we know,' explained Wilbur, glancing at James, 'and well, Chad,' he took a step towards him, 'you've been a vampire longer than any of us combined. You wouldn't sell us out. You've seen civilisations rise and fall, you've lived through countless historical wars. No, you would never betray us.'

'I'll just tell them the family crisis is still ongoing,' Rachel's voice came through from the corridor as she and Keisuke entered the cabin.

'We're going to have to go back to work eventually, though,' Keisuke replied, as the two of them emerged from the foyer and entered the sitting room, 'and we need a good story for when we do, because Andrew—' Keisuke stopped, a hesitant look upon his face.

Stella and Wilbur glared at them wide-eyed.

'You brought mortals!?' Stella shrieked.

'It's okay!' Rachel raised her hands in surrender. 'I'm Liam's sister.'

'And I'm the boyfriend,' said Keisuke, pointing a thumb in Rachel's direction.

'They've been helping us and lodging us since that night at the estate,' explained Liam. 'You can trust them.'

'Can we, though?' Wilbur walked right up to Keisuke and stared into his eyes as the two tall men faced off. Removing the glasses he wore for show, the elder vampire flared his eyes. Keisuke reacted, startled, but he didn't back down from the staredown or step back. 'Wilbur bared his fangs at him.'

'Hey, hands off!' Rachel slapped Wilbur's arm. She placed her hands on her hips. 'I gave my blood to save Julian's life when my brother, Chad and James brought him into my house. It was *my* tweezers that got a silver bullet out of him. We got them food and blood, and we got *shot at!* So your teeth don't scare me, but *please* can you treat us like we're not lesser just because we're mortals.'

'She's right,' Liam spoke up. 'It's thanks to her we're all in one piece. And Keisuke.'

'Very well, I'll allow it,' began Wilbur, 'but if you so much as slap me again—'

'Then what?' Rachel folded her arms, unimpressed.

A smile curled on Wilbur's mouth. He turned to Liam. 'I like her, she doesn't back down.' Returning his glasses to his face, he turned back to Rachel, his tone now polite and amiable. 'Apologies, I had to be certain of your intentions.'

'Wait, was that a test?' her face scrunched into an annoyed expression. 'Ugh! Vampires.'

Chuckling, Wilbur took her hand and gave it a gentleman's kiss.

'Uh, excuse me?' Keisuke interjected, stepping up beside Rachel, who blushed and laughed self-consciously.

Wilbur stepped back and turned to the group, reassuming a serious demeanour. He clapped his hands together, rubbing them. 'All right, enough pre-amble. Stella and I both received the same message, sent to us the night things went down at the club.'

Everyone shifted uneasily.

Wilbur motioned to a computer on the table. 'It was encrypted.'

'That's Zack's work, then,' deduced Chad.

Wilbur nodded. 'We've finally been able to decrypt it, after several failed attempts. We have not yet viewed it.'

'We wanted to include you,' Stella continued. 'We felt we might be able to better assess the situation together.'

'Have Zack and Zanitha come in contact with either of you, then?' Chad asked earnestly.

Stella shook her head. 'Aside from the encrypted message, nothing. We considered messaging them, but since the encryption came *from them,* perhaps it would compromise their position if we did.'

'Then let's play it,' Julian adjured. 'Let's see what they have that was so important they had to encrypt it before sending it.'

Wilbur nodded. Everyone gathered around to stand beside him to look at the screen as he let the video message play.

A webcam gave a view of Zanitha sitting at the computer, recording her screen while she spoke. On the computer, processes were running – the encryption, Liam surmised. Behind her, Zack pressed his back against a door, both hands holding his handgun up near his face, his expression hardened and resolved.

'We've found something,' Zanitha said gravely. 'It's . . . not good. You need to hear it for yourselves. It's currently encrypting and should be done soon.

Should . . . the people in question get their hands on this file or attempt to erase it, they'll fail the attempt and won't be able to know what's on here.'

The door budged and Zack pressed against it harder. 'I can't hold this for much longer. Let's hope that thing gets sent before they come through.'

'It's really bad,' Zanitha went on, her eyes wide with fear. 'It's not just mobs coming after us, but cops too, someone at the top of their ranks. We . . . The Cromwells found a recording between someone and a government appointee, between a *vampire* and—'

The door burst open, sending Zack staggering back. He shot the mobsters that poured into the room, but more kept coming – for a vampire's strength to fail here, there had to be a lot of humans.

Chad shook his head. 'No,' he breathed. 'Shit!'

James put a hand on his shoulder. Liam glanced from Chad to Julian and back at the screen.

'We have a mole,' Zanitha warned. 'And the person who's betrayed us . . . it's—'

Zack screamed as a bullet hit him and he staggered back, always shooting, even as he fell to the floor onto his side. Zack's face contorted in pain and his body went limp as blood spilled from a shoulder wound whose inky tendrils snaked outward on his exposed flesh.

Zanitha turned to stare at her twin, shock and fear in her eyes, then back at the screen. 'It's—'

Liam shut his eyes at the horror, turning to bury his face in Julian's chest – Zanitha had been shot in the head. Liam saw that Rachel and Keisuke had already turned away from the screen, their hushed voices indicating they had not seen the gruesomeness but had anticipated it.

'I think I'm going to be sick,' muttered Chad.

'She was about to tell us who it was,' Julian quavered. 'She knew, Zack and Zanitha knew who betrayed us.'

The blood-spattered webcam continued to show the bloody scene as someone hunkered over to the computer. The encryption completed – the recording showed that much – and the program instantly sent the message, confirming its envoy. Then everything went dead.

Silence fell on the group.

'That was the video file,' Stella said softly. 'We have the audio file that came with it, which we also just decrypted.' She waited.

Chad put a hand to his mouth, staring at the screen in horror. He spun and sped out the door.

James turned as if to follow; Julian stopped him. 'Give him a few.'

'I'll go,' Liam advised.

He found Chad standing just outside a few paces from the walkway and looking up at the sky. 'Hey,' he said gently.

'Oh god,' breathed Chad. 'Liam I . . . they're gone, they're really gone, this time it happened for real.'

Liam walked over to him and put a gentle hand on his shoulder, the man already had tears pouring down his face.

'I'm so sorry, Chad. I know you loved them.' He hesitated. He thought about adding something more but refrained, for the words felt hollow.

'It never gets easy, you know. You'd think after losing so many people I'd grow a thick skin, but no, no matter who it is, it hurts to lose someone I care for, someone I love. And now I've lost someone again, in double . . . double the pain.'

Liam didn't know what to say as the other vampire sobbed, so he gently wrapped his arms around him and felt Chad collapse into his embrace.

'Oh my god, Liam, they're dead.'

'I know.' Liam stroked the top of Chad's head, like he would his sister's when she was weeping in his arms. He might not have known Chad as long as the others, but they had all grown close over the months. They were friends, roommates, they were his coven, and it hurt to see someone he cared about in such pain.

After a moment, Chad pulled away. 'And I've gone and done it again, I've fallen in love with someone, only to lose them in the end because that's what's going to happen.'

'You're not going to lose me,' asserted James, appearing at the doorway.

Liam looked up as Chad turned around, wiping his face with his hand. James walked up to him.

'You won't lose me,' James repeated, 'at least not for a long while.' He smiled in sympathy, wiping Chad's tears with his thumbs. 'Hey, baby, we're going to figure this out, okay, the whole vampire-werewolf thing, because I've fallen in love with you too.'

Chad let out a sobbed laugh and they kissed tenderly, their lips opening for more of each other's mouths as they stayed in this moment for a bit longer before pulling apart.

Chad looked at Liam. 'Hey, thanks, eh.'

'Anytime, Chad.' Liam pointed a thumb in the direction of the door. 'We should probably get back and hear the rest of what Zack and Zanitha wanted us to hear.'

Chad nodded, looking resolved.

Back inside, the others wore sympathetic smiles, but Chad dismissed them with a wave of his hand and a soft, 'I'm good. We're ready for what comes next.'

'If you're certain,' said Stella. She turned to Wilbur. 'Let's proceed to the audio file the twins sent us.'

The audio began between two people. The voices were altered through tech, making it difficult to distinguish one from the other, apart from the fact that one voice had a flatter tone, while the other had a more melodic quality. It was like listening to a horror movie's murderer's voice.

'I have to admit, I'm surprised at how well things have progressed so far,' one voice said.

'Didn't I tell you to trust me?' the flatter voice replied. 'I told you I was in a position where I could help.'

'I know, but it's hard to tell which human is going to get in the way next,' the other voice complained.

The second person chuckled. 'Yes, many humans become obstacles. But I have you to thank for helping me rise to where I am today.'

'I promised I'd get you the D.C. position and I did.'

'Even if I'm just a human?'

'You're one of the special ones, Anthony.'

There was a pause in the audio, as though both were taking the time to think.

'Anthony Whitlock, Deputy Chief for the police force,' said Wilbur. 'I am not surprised. We have confirmation now.'

'What about the others of your kind?' asked who Liam presumed was the D.C.

'Let *me* handle them. I have an ace up my sleeve.'

'And by ace up your sleeve you mean me,' corrected Anthony Whitlock.

'Whatevs.' There was a giggle.

Liam's blood ran cold. He recognised the expression. Julian beside him tensed, and Chad's face twisted in rage.

'I'll be in touch with instructions.'

'Understood.'

Their call ended.

Chad leaned forward, gripping the back of a chair, seething. 'I'm going to kill that bitch.'

Stella and Wilbur's expressions remained inscrutable. 'We have to be wise about this,' Stella cautioned.

'I'm going to fucking kill her!' shouted Chad, pushing away from the chair. '*Maledictum in eam!*'

Julian placed a hand on Chad's shoulder. 'We need to think this through rationally.'

'Rationally?' Chad whirled on Julian and shoved him. 'You want me to calm down when a vampire I trusted – one I took under my wing, one I cared for like a sister – killed people I loved! Betrayed our coven! And caused the deaths of so many of our kind! You want me to think rationally?!'

'Chad, you know what I mean,' warned Julian, his voice rising.

'Uh,' Rachel began hesitantly, 'who was the vampire speaking to the D.C.?'

'Mandy!' growled Chad. With a sharp spin, he fixed his gaze on Rachel, getting in her face. 'That bitch betrayed us and got Zack and Zanitha killed.'

'Chad,' warned Rachel, 'please take a step back. You're not angry at *me*.'

Liam walked over and placed a hand on Chad's shoulder, gently pulling him away from his sister. Rachel was not afraid but she looked uncomfortable, and Keisuke looked ready to pounce on the vampire if need be. That being said, Liam also knew that they trusted Chad and understood he was merely trying to release his anger.

'I'm sorry, Rachel,' Chad whispered, bowing his head.

She smiled in sympathy and placed two hands on his arms, rubbing soothingly, slowly. 'We need to figure out why she would do such a thing. Find out what motivates her in order to figure out her next step so we can catch her, so that you *can* kill her without putting the rest of your coven in danger. We need to think like detectives.'

Chad scowled, looking puzzled.

'Sorry, I read a lot of true crime. You say you knew her well, Chad, what can you tell me about her? Perhaps a human's perspective can help.'

Chad smiled despite himself. He looked at Liam. 'Your sister's good at comforting. Okay,' he took a few steps back, thinking. 'Mandy became part of our coven in the early 1800s.'

'When and how?' asked Rachel.

'The circumstances behind her turning are unusual,' began Wilbur, 'and she was our only exception once the coven was established. In the late 17th Century, there was a man who learnt about us and wanted to be turned. At the time we did not know it but he went under the guise of several aliases. He was a murderer and had a bloodlust to see people bleed and suffer.'

'When we turned him,' explained Stella, 'he seemed overexcited, and we soon learnt about his murderous ways. He would kill using his vampire skills; tear people apart or bite them and then watch them bleed until the fear in their eyes left them lifeless.'

'But he got careless,' continued Chad, 'and Mandy was one such careless error. He watched her bleed only to see her turn. We were hunting him when we found her – frightened and hiding, her skin already reacting to the sun with boils developing into a rash. She didn't know we were vampires and she tried to attack us. I subdued her and helped her calm down. That's when she told us her story.'

Chad closed his eyes. 'She was a young woman, just barely twenty, already a mother of two – a son and a daughter – children she was wrenched from and would never see again.'

Remaining silent, Keisuke pulled out his phone and began tapping away and scrolling.

'So there is resentment, anger, regret,' said Rachel. 'What happened to the murderous vampire?'

'We staked him,' said Stella. 'Thanks to Mandy's details and exceptional memory, we found his trail, tracked him down, and he took a stake to the heart.' She sighed. 'I bonded with her over our similar fates, except when I was attacked and turned, I had already lived fifty years of my life.'

Stella's expression grew sad as she looked at Chad's tormented face. 'Chad was there to find and help me when *I* was turned. That was much, much longer ago, and since then our coven's rule has always been to turn others with their *explicit consent only.*'

'It was a rule many of us . . . more ancient vampires established,' expressed Chad, 'a rule I advocated for nearly immediately after I became a vampire, a rule I had hoped all other vampires would have adopted by now.'

'Seeing as I came to be grateful for becoming a vampire,' Stella went on, 'I thought Mandy would get over what had happened. And for a time, we all thought she had.'

'She fooled us all,' sighed Wilbur. His eyes grew distant as he recounted the memory. 'I found her unconscious in the sun one time. I saved her, not realising she had attempted to kill herself, but she wasn't angry with me, she merely said it was fate, and from that moment on, she was her peppy self.'

'I taught Mandy everything there was to know about being a vampire,' said Chad, his brows creased in chagrin. 'I was her mentor, her older brother. As times changed, we always adapted our style, our speech, she the most, and together we would go shopping. I had her pose as a rich widow and me as her butler many times. We had so much fun with roleplay like that. I thought she had finally gotten over everything, for she appeared to be happy again.'

A tear ran down Chad's cheek. 'I trusted her. I cared about her and I thought she felt the same way about me. I thought she regarded me as her older brother. I guess I was wrong.'

James wrapped his strong arms around Chad and the vampire wept in the werewolf's caress.

'I'm guessing she wasn't always named Mandy?' Keisuke piped up.

'No,' replied Wilbur. 'Mandy was her latest alteration.'

'I started calling her Mandy,' said Chad, still in James's arms, his head leaning on the werewolf's broad shoulder. 'I started calling her Mandy before the name Mandy became popular.'

'What was her original name?' asked Keisuke.

'Magdalen,' replied Chad. 'Why?'

'Magdalen Boyd?'

Chad scowled, pulling away from James. 'Yes, why? What have you found?'

Keisuke lifted his phone's screen and turned it around towards the others.

'What are we looking at, Keisuke?' asked Julian.

'It's an app that allows you to look into genealogy and the historically recorded names of celebrities and other public figures.' Keisuke looked back at his screen. 'I looked into the D.C.'s background.

'In his family tree, from the early eighteen hundreds is a Magdalen Boyd, married to a Christopher Alexander Whitlock, with a son and a daughter. It says that Magdalen Boyd disappeared under mysterious circumstances and her body was never found though she was presumed dead. A series of strange murders was uncovered shortly after and they assumed she had been one of these murder victims.'

'Which she was,' Chad murmured.

Keisuke showed everyone his phone again. 'According to these results, which are public information, Mandy is the D.C.'s ancestor. He's her family.'

A silence fell on the group.

'Could she have wished she had not been turned and now wants to get back at all vampires for what happened to her?' suggested Rachel.

'But we only helped her!' insisted Chad.

'Maybe, but to her, she was forced into a life she did not choose,' said Liam. 'When I first arrived at the manor, the first thing Wilbur asked Julian was to confirm that I had consented before I was turned. Mandy never consented, she was turned against her will and then thrown into this life.' Liam motioned to

Keisuke's phone. 'If you ask me, it seems we found motive beyond any reasonable doubt.'

'She's working with humans to eliminate vampires because she wishes she was still a human,' concluded Rachel. 'She wants vampires exterminated so that no one ever has to go through what she went through, and to get revenge. And she's getting help from her family, from those who are her flesh and blood, no matter how many centuries removed they are.'

'Perhaps we've figured that out,' began Wilbur, 'but that still doesn't solve our problem of figuring out her next move . . . or ours.'

'Isn't it obvious?' Keisuke declared. 'The vampires and werewolves have to work together.'

Everyone gaped at him as though he were an alien who'd just grown tentacles out of his head.

'I understand you wish to help, Keisuke,' began James, 'but you don't seem to understand the centuries-old war and rivalry between werewolves and vampires.'

'It's time to set that aside, though,' insisted Keisuke, looking from James to the vampires, conviction in his voice and eyes. 'There's no going forward without both sides helping each other. Mandy's actions have already affected both your coven *and* your pack.'

Rachel blushed, smiling. 'You okay there, sister?' Liam asked quietly enough.

'Isn't he just so sexy when he gets all . . .'

Liam had to admit, as he watched Keisuke lay his arguments down to James and the other vampires, that he looked very much in his element. 'Yeah,' he agreed.

'No offence, but a mere mortal human, who understands little of our history, will not and cannot get the heads of some of the largest vampire covens and werewolf packs to agree to cooperate,' insisted Wilbur.

Keisuke chuckled into his fist before looking even more resolved. 'I don't think you understand. I've been the Head of the Sales department for the past five years and at the same company for the past ten. There is a reason why I moved up in rank so fast and so high.' He leaned forward, grinning. 'I always close a deal I'm negotiating for. And when I say I always close a deal, I mean *every* . . . single . . . deal. No exceptions.'

'But they'll never agree—' began James.

'You leave that to me, James,' Keisuke interrupted.

'They're not coming here,' Wilbur warned.

'I'll find us a meeting room,' Keisuke assured. 'I just need to have your pack' – he looked at James, then at Wilbur – 'and your coven – well the leaders – in the same room, and I promise you, *I will close this deal.*' His grin widened and his eyes lit up with passion. 'Guaranteed.'

Wilbur and Stella sat facing Adrienne and Martin, next to the Alphas was James. Across from him sat Chad, with Julian beside him, and next to Julian was Liam. Rachel sat at the far end of the table, typing notes on a laptop that was connected to a printer.

Keisuke stood at the head of the table, looking very sharp with his glasses on.

After having discussed the plan with Stella and Wilbur, James had called his pack leaders. Keisuke had presented himself as an associate of James's, which wasn't far from the truth.

When Adrienne and Martin first walked in, they sniffed Keisuke, eyes flashing as they used their abilities to enhance their sense of smell, and snorted in complaint.

'We're here to discuss with a human?' Adrienne insulted Keisuke. 'You are but a human.'

'Yes,' Keisuke had diplomatically agreed. 'You would have far more serious problems on your hands if I were of an alien species.' And he flashed a polite smile. 'Please, have a seat.'

The werewolves had complied, and now the two groups were attempting to negotiate terms that would suit and benefit both the werewolf pack and the vampire coven moving forward. The two factions were the largest in the area for miles around – they held the power to shape the destiny of smaller covens and packs regions out. Their decision today would ripple through the continent and impact the entire world of Underworld beings, with the potential to negotiate peace and forge a strong new alliance.

As Keisuke had instructed them to do, Stella and Wilbur were reticent in putting forward any concessions when he asked them, 'What are you willing to compromise?' Instead, insisting they were willing to compromise nothing. They played their part well to give the impression that the accommodations they did make were viewed as fair without letting the werewolves take more than they themselves were offering.

James had agreed to this plan, propounding that if the vampires seemed to give in first, the werewolves would be more amenable to suggesting compromises in return.

'Now, now, we discussed this earlier,' Keisuke put forth, his face giving nothing away to the plan, 'you have to be willing to give something up if you want the werewolves to meet you halfway.'

'Fine,' Stella sighed dramatically. 'We will cease any and all hostilities with any and all werewolves and speak with other vampire covens to negotiate that other werewolf packs and vampire covens can eventually come to an agreement as well.'

'I suppose it's only fair that we do the same,' voiced Adrienne. 'Of course, if we successfully work together, then it may set an example.' She took a beat. 'We will need the vampires to make amends.'

'As the vampires will need the werewolves to do,' Wilbur purveyed. 'But we cannot think about making amends so long as a mafia and the D.C. are after both our coven and pack.'

'What about your betrayer?' demanded Martin.

'She will get what's coming to her,' seethed Chad. 'She got vampires killed, and we deal with betrayal of that kind with death.'

Adrienne and Martin seemed pleased with Chad's genuine response.

'There is one more thing that might help us agree,' began Adrienne.

Keisuke had predicted some of their demands based on what James had told him, and Keisuke had negotiated with Stella and Wilbur to allow some exceptions. Keisuke had also spoken to other elders of the coven over the phone and had convinced them as well. When laying out his arguments before the werewolf and vampire leaders, he reiterated many points he had made to both groups individually.

Everyone knew what demand Adrienne was going to put forth now.

'We would like to take over the city,' stated Adrienne. 'Everything the Cromwells control. Since we have already posed as a mafia in charge of many aspects and facilities in the city, we want free reign without the interference of the vampires. In return, we will let you continue as you have, and we may . . . then . . . see about coexisting in this way.'

Stella and Wilbur hesitated, though Keisuke had already convinced them that such a demand would be to their benefit and how this would be the expected best possible outcome. He had informed them that if this was to be presented as the werewolves' demands, then they should jump on it.

Julian was impressed with the man and truly understood why he closed every single deal he negotiated for. Now sitting at this conference table in the middle of the night, Julian had a new admiration for Liam's brother-in-law. Both Keisuke and Rachel had helped them so much already. They were incredible humans, and Julian loved his fiancé's sister more by the minute, so grateful was he towards her. His heart swelled for Liam in that moment, eager to see Keisuke work his magic.

Liam must have sensed Julian's excitement, for he took his hand, smiling.

'Fine,' sighed Stella. 'We agree to your terms.'

But the werewolves still hesitated, reluctant to sign into an alliance with vampires.

'Listen,' said Keisuke, 'do you want to let humans dictate the rest of your lives? I know there's been war between your kind for centuries, but do you each want to sit back and let humans dictate your future?' His tone grew more inspiring, 'Or do you want to begin a new era where werewolves and vampires alike shape the world as you want it to be?!'

Now he spoke with such conviction, Julian wanted to sign any and all contracts he'd present to him.

'Show me what an era where vampires and werewolves working together looks like. Show me how a future run by the beings of the Underworld can benefit our world.' Keisuke pointed at himself – 'Show this human,' – he opened his arms out, as though motioning the world – 'show *all* humans, before they even know you exist, of the great future that awaits humanity and all your kin if you agree to this new alliance today.'

Keisuke narrowed his eyes. 'It's time to incite an evolution, not a revolution.' He placed his hands on the table and leaned towards the werewolves. 'You have the power to shape the world like it is putty in your hands. *You* have that power, here, today, right now, to change the course of the future, and *make it yours*!'

Adrienne smirked. She stood, as did Martin, and both extended their hands towards the vampires. Stella and Wilbur stood as well, and the werewolf and vampire leaders shook hands. Chad and James exchanged a knowing smile.

Keisuke clapped his hands together. 'Excellent.' He looked up at Rachel who finished typing something up. Then the printer printed the documents.

Keisuke walked over and stapled the documents together. He placed them on the table. 'Please sign here, here, and here. One copy for the werewolves, one for the vampires, and one for me.' Keisuke then signed the three documents. 'This guarantees my non-disclosure.'

'Does it also guarantee you'll be present during our negotiations for both sides to make amends?' asked Martin, cocking a brow.

Keisuke grinned. 'It's already been laid out in clause 5-B.'

'Then hand me that pen, good human!' chuckled Martin.

James let out an obvious sigh of relief.

The vampires and werewolves signed the documents, making their agreement final. Keisuke smiled with pride. Julian had to hand it to him; he did it, he truly closed this deal and got vampires and werewolves to work together as fellow kin.

'Now,' said Keisuke, taking a seat, 'let's begin figuring out our strategy.'

* * *

'Come on, vampires!' Rachel barked, looking on at the vampires and werewolves training and sparring. 'I've seen mere mortals move faster than that! You're slow. I want to see blurs, not sluggishness.'

Liam stopped what he was doing and turned to his sister, chuckling. 'God, Rachel, you're annoying, you know that, right?'

She shrugged. Liam laughed. He wiped the sweat from his forehead and came to sit beside her. Placing his elbows on his knees, he leaned forward, catching his breath.

'They're grilling me hard, training me real good, but I feel I can do this, get at least up to level to some of the younger vampires.'

'When you say younger,' began Rachel, eyeing some children and teenagers doing moves with such speed they were a blur even to Liam.

'I mean vampires who were turned more recently,' Liam clarified.

After the Sharpes and the coven had signed into the new alliance, everyone agreed to train and prepare to fight the humans under the command of D.C. Whitlock. The werewolves had agreed to allow vampires at one of their bases of operations – a large warehouse just outside the city. Right next to it was a hotel run by the Sharpes, and tonight, all the rooms were going to be occupied by vampires and werewolves only.

The vampire elders had gotten in touch with other vampires, asking the usual to find out who was with whom and where. Those they could trust the most were told more details before arriving here. Others learnt about Mandy when they arrived.

Stella had contacted Mandy and told her to wait for further instructions. Liam didn't know much of the details but they were planning to send someone specially trained to kill other vampires to take her out.

Chad and James were training together, co-ordinating attacks, other werewolves were in one corner of the large room, while vampires were training here and there throughout the building. Julian had gone to speak with Stella and Wilbur in private.

Rachel placed a hand on Liam's back, rubbing. 'I'm very proud of you, you know.' She smiled and Liam leaned towards her for a side hug, opening his arms to wrap them around her.

'Ew, stinky.' Rachel put a hand to her mouth, her face paling.

'Come on, it's not that bad.'

'Sorry, I gotta go.' She stood and ran towards the washroom.

Worried, Liam followed. He waited a bit before speaking through the door. 'Rachel, are you okay?' He gently pushed the door open. Rachel was splashing water on her face.

'Yeah, I'm fine.'

Liam scowled. 'You're not fine. You just puked.' He could smell the lingering vomit in the air. Rachel shifted. Liam approached her and put a hand on her arm. 'Are you sick?'

'I didn't want to worry you with everything going on but . . .' She nervously chewed her lip.

'Oh my god, Rachel, just tell me what's going on. I'm worried about you.'

Rachel smiled fondly and placed a hand on his face, cupping his cheek. 'I'm not sick, Liam. I . . . Let's just say you're not the only one I need to look out for anymore.'

Liam's eyes widened and his mouth hung open as he realised what Rachel was saying. 'Oh my god, Rachel, you're pregnant!'

She beamed and laughed lightly. 'Yes, I'm pregnant.'

'Does Keisuke know?'

Rachel nodded. 'He knows.'

Liam hugged his sister. 'I'm so happy for you!' They exited the washroom and made their way back to the main room.

Keisuke hurried to Rachel's side, looking concerned. He placed a hand on her stomach as he began to fuss over her. 'I told you, you shouldn't be overexerting yourself.'

'I'm not overexerting myself, Kei, I'm shouting at vampires to keep them motivated.' She giggled. 'It's actually quite fun.'

Keisuke began rubbing her shoulders gently as the two walked off together. It was heartwarming to see them together and to see Keisuke taking care of Rachel like that.

Liam continued towards the door that gave access to the corridor that led to the room where Julian was still having his discussion with Stella and Wilbur. He stopped when he noticed Victoria and Richard walking towards him.

'Victoria?' She waved at him as he joined her. 'What are you doing here?'

'Helping.' She smiled. 'While everyone was staying off the radar, Richard and I were busy – weren't we, sweetheart?'

'Yes, my darling.'

'Wait, are you two . . . ?' asked Liam.

Victoria blushed and smiled. 'We are.' She and Richard exchanged a flirtatious smile. 'He's a bit older but he's not going to age. After what happened at the club – not my best moment, let's forget that ever happened – he explained everything to me, and I decided I wanted to help and I just happened to know how.'

She grinned, folding her arms and holding her head up with the pride Liam recognised she often held herself with. It was comforting to see her back to her usual self, especially after what had happened at the club.

'Right, so when you say you were busy,' began Liam, smirking cheekily.

'Well, there was some of that too, of course.' Victoria let out a shy laugh, flicking a lock of blonde hair back. Richard blushed bashfully, which was alluring for a man his age.

'How's that going, then, with Richard a vampire?'

'Same as you and Julian now, I imagine.' Victoria grinned at Liam. Her eyes flared and her canines extended.

Liam's jaw dropped. 'No way! Victoria! Richard turned you?'

Victoria laughed. 'Yeah. I asked him to. I gave it some thought and I decided it's what I wanted. Besides, the club's now got a co-owner – the Sharpes and I are keeping our previous agreement in place. It's all working out for the better.' She glanced at Richard. 'In addition to all that, the Mayor of our city is a childhood friend of mine. He's agreed to help.'

'You told him about the vampires and werewolves!'

'Mayor Hayes is on our side,' said Richard, 'and on his way here now.'

'Wait, can you trust him?' demanded Liam.

'He's been vetted,' Richard assured.

'Not sure what that means but I'll trust you, you are, after all, an elder,' said Liam. Richard was also one of the three coven leaders, Liam reminded himself.

'Speaking of the man.' Richard pointed towards the door at the far end where in walked Mayor Mitchell Hayes, smirking with pride. A hush fell on the room; Adrienne, Martin, James and Chad approached him.

Liam followed a grinning Victoria and Richard to join them. Victoria embraced the Mayor. He turned to the werewolves.

'Missus Sharpe, Mister Sharpe,' he acknowledged them. 'I have a proposition.' His smile was suave. 'As it happens, we have a common enemy. Deputy Chief Anthony Whitlock has been a thorn in my side for years. I am willing to help you take out the Cromwells and expose Whitlock's dirty secrets to discharge him of his duties and responsibilities and get him off your backs for good.'

Adrienne eyed him carefully. 'Okay, sounds nice in theory. What do *you* get by helping us?'

'Cleaning up the streets of my city will help get me re-elected. During my second term, I can train my successor to ensure the people vote that person into office after my term has ended,' he inclined his head forward, 'a successor who could very well be a Sharpe.'

Martin guffawed. 'You're going to get one of us to be elected as Mayor? How does that benefit you? How can we trust you?'

Hayes flashed them a grin. 'In return for my help and alliance, I want you to make me one of you.'

The werewolves eyed him carefully. 'One of us?' asked James.

'I want you to make me a werewolf.'

James gaped at the man, eyes wide. 'Are you serious?'

'I most certainly am! I won't be Mayor forever, and if my successor is a Sharpe, we can guarantee to take proper care of the city while ensuring those suspecting vampires and werewolves exist don't find out.' He leaned forward. 'Humans and you need to work together, and I want in by becoming one of you. I can help eliminate those who would secretly spread word of your existence – legally, of course – and get those to whom they would speak about it on *our* side before they even *learn* of your existence.'

'Just hear him out,' advised Richard. 'What he has to say is very interesting.'

'Perhaps we can discuss this in private, then,' suggested Adrienne.

'Certainly.'

'Well, first off,' Adrienne began as they started off, 'you'll have to wait until the next full moon to be turned. A werewolf turning can only happen during Feral Night.'

Hayes rubbed his chin. 'I suppose that gives me time to grow a beard. I reckon the new look might suit me.'

Martin chuckled. 'You might fit right in, in that case.' He clapped the Mayor on the back while twirling his well-groomed beard with his other hand.

Victoria gave a finger wave to Liam before following Richard, Mayor Hayes, and the Sharpe leaders into a private room, leaving Liam standing on his own.

He turned and walked along the corridor towards the room where he heard Julian and Wilbur's raised voices.

'Be reasonable, Julian!' came Wilbur's voice.

'Why can't Chad do it?' demanded Julian.

'He's too close to it, he'll give himself away as soon as she sees him.'

'So that leaves me?!' shouted Julian.

Liam discretely entered the room to find Wilbur and Julian standing face to face, both wore stern looks on their faces.

Julian seethed, his voice barely a whisper. 'You seem to forget I'm not the only one who this will affect if it fails.'

'Julian you're the only one I trust to do it, the one with the skill, the one I trained for just this very thing.' Wilbur sighed. 'Considering the circumstances, you're the only one we believe can pull this off.'

Julian clenched his teeth, staring at the ground. 'Fine.'

'What's going on?' Liam asked carefully.

'Liam!' Julian stared at him in shock. Then he glared at Wilbur. He stalked off – Liam followed.

'Julian, what's going on?' Julian kept on walking angrily. Liam hurried to keep up. 'Julian, talk to me.'

Julian pushed past a set of double doors, slamming both of them open with such force the noise echoed in the corridor.

'Please tell me what this is about,' Liam pressed, as they exited the building and walked a small path towards the hotel.

Julian gave no reply, he merely kept on into the hotel and up a set of stairs.

'What the hell, Julian! Don't ignore me!'

Julian stopped abruptly. He worked his jaw, mouth closed, before resuming towards one of the rooms. Julian marched right into the dark room. Liam shut the door behind them.

The moon outside cast an indigo glow within the room. Liam's heart was pounding, he felt so confused.

Julian spun to face Liam, and the blond man could see the glint of tears in Julian's eyes. 'I promise I'm not ignoring you! I . . .'

Julian paused and Liam saw a similar look on his face as the night Liam almost died.

'Liam, do you remember the first time we made love? The *very* first time?'

'Of course. You drove me nuts the way you were rubbing yourself on me. Nearly made me come sucking me.' Liam smiled at the memory, feeling himself blush. 'You had me take you from behind while you shouted out the open window.'

'Yeah,' Julian chuckled but his eyes reflected sadness, 'that was so you wouldn't see my eyes flare or my canines extend. Our first time together was so intense, so magnificent, so mind-blowing, I could barely control my instincts.'

'And then I grabbed you and pumped you.'

'And we came together,' they both completed.

'Before getting it on again and again the whole night,' added Liam.

Julian took a step towards him. 'Let's do it again. I want to make love to you like that, just like our first time.'

'Why? I mean I've no objections, but what's brought this on?' asked Liam, concerned. Julian looked down. 'Julian, what's going on?'

The silence was suffocating, the same way it had been after Julian had disappeared. When Julian spoke, his voice was grave, and Liam could hear the fear in his voice. 'Wilbur's asked me to be the one to contact Mandy.'

Liam waited to hear more, yet something about the admission shook him to his core.

'Says I'm the best one for it – Chad would give himself away.'

'Okay,' Liam replied carefully, 'best one for what?'

Julian turned his back to Liam and walked a few steps towards the window. 'Whoever gets in touch with her will meet with her.'

Liam began to put two and two together and his heart sank with sudden dread.

Julian turned to face Liam again. 'Liam, I'm going to kill her.' Liam nodded carefully. 'I need to catch her by surprise, sell my story, but chances are she's going to fight me.'

Liam felt himself tremble.

Julian creased his brows in sadness. 'I'm the bait. Liam,' Julian whispered, his voice wet as he struggled to contain his tears. 'There is a chance she might kill me.'

Liam's heart squeezed and he felt like he couldn't breathe.

'And if not her, the D.C.'s squad might.'

Liam merely stared at Julian for a long time.

'Why did you accept?' Liam hissed, his voice low and dangerous. 'Why did you accept the task?'

'Because I was trained to kill other vampires if it came to such things,' replied Julian. 'Not everyone knows how, it's a special skill, and of those who know, well, I'm the best one for this mission.'

Liam felt his fear mount. 'And why can't anyone else go with you?'

'It's a very tricky situation, given the circumstances. I'm the only one that won't give it away if it's me who goes to meet her.'

'So that's what you were shouting about with Wilbur?' Liam heard the anger rise in his voice.

'Yes.' Julian took a step towards Liam and placed his hand on his face.

Liam turned his face away. 'Don't!' He took a step back.

'Liam, please, don't be like that.'

'Like what?' snapped Liam. 'Angry that my fiancé accepted to risk his life and die when he's supposed to be promising his life to me?' His breath was shaking. 'You're supposed to be putting me first!' he yelled. 'We're supposed to be writing vows and spending the rest of our lives together!'

'Liam,' Julian pleaded, 'I need you right now, please.'

'What about *me* needing *you*, Julian, huh?' Now, he screamed, 'What about me needing you *for the rest of my life!*' Both let out loud sobs. Julian looked tormented but Liam was too angry to stop shouting. 'You turned me into an immortal vampire, for what, to die a few months later? Is that your way of getting out of marrying me?'

'No!' cried Julian. 'How could you even think that? I want to spend the rest of my life with you! I love you.' He heaved, hands reaching towards Liam before dropping them to his sides again, pleading silently.

Liam raised his left hand, presenting the back of his hand and spreading out his fingers and letting the moonlight glint on his ring. 'Eternally yours,' he whispered. 'Was it all a lie?' he disdained, his voice barely audible.

Tears began to flow freely from Julian's eyes. 'Liam, please. I know I can do this but I'm scared and I need you right now.'

'I need you, Julian,' yelled Liam, still holding his hand up, 'I need you *forever*, but because you agreed to this,' – he balled his hand into a tight fist – 'we might not *have* forever.'

Julian winced like he'd been punched in the gut.

Dropping his fist to his side, Liam seethed. 'Maybe you should have let me die that night.'

Liam regretted it as soon as he said it. He closed his eyes tightly, feeling his own tears sting his eyes. He looked up to see Julian sobbing heavily.

'Do you truly wish that?' Julian whispered through sobs.

'I don't want to live in a world without you, Julian.' Liam's voice cracked even as he wept. 'I'm sorry I shouted, Julian, I'm just so scared. I don't want to lose you. But I'm here for you, I'm here and I'm not going anywhere because I love you, I'm in love with you, and I'll always be here for you, eternally, because my love for you *is eternal.*'

Julian marched to Liam and grabbed his face in his hands, kissing him desperately, their tears mingling on both their faces.

Liam felt pang after pang as his heart ached for Julian, all while a desperate need rose within him. He felt his canines extend and he didn't fight it. As he fervently kissed his lover, smacking his lips against his, Julian's canines also extended.

Julian sobbed into Liam's mouth as Liam moaned. Their lips parted only enough for them to grab air before they pressed themselves against each other again.

Liam tugged on Julian's clothes and Julian pulled on his. Letting their coats drop to the floor, and reaching under his shirt, Liam pressed his hands against Julian's skin. He lifted and pulled his lover's shirt off.

He paused, taking a step back, staring at Julian's tear-stricken face. Liam removed his shirt, pulling it over his head, and let it fall to the floor. Julian took a step forward, placing his warm hands on Liam's chest. He kissed the tears on Liam's cheek, but even as he did, his eyes shut tight and more tears came to wet both their faces.

Gliding his hands down, Liam reached for Julian's pants. As though wanting to make each moment last longer, they slowly undid each other's belts and pulled down. Liam's pants dropped to the floor and he stepped out of them. Julian did the same and Liam admired the body of the man he loved, this body that so aroused him and made him lose all senses.

Julian took a step forward and Liam a step back. With a hand on his chest, Julian walked Liam back towards the bed. Liam sat on it, wanting to take his fiancé's hard and plump cock in his mouth. Julian placed a knee on the bed, pushing Liam onto his back.

Interlacing their fingers, Julian and Liam clasped both hands as they continued to desperately devour each other's mouths, always hungry for more, as they always were when they made love.

Julian began to slide up and down Liam's length, his erection rubbing against the other vampire's. Liam moaned gutturally, tightening his grip on Julian's hands. Julian kissed Liam's neck, his collarbone, his pectoral – he took a nibble, his canines tingling Liam's skin. Liam's entire body throbbed from the sensation it elicited.

A wave of pleasure hit Liam and he cried out his elation, and then sobbed Julian's name.

Julian lowered himself some more, letting go of Liam's hands. His shaft pressed against Liam's balls as Julian thrust forward before rubbing on his perineum.

'Oh, god, Julian.' Liam moaned.

Julian lowered himself completely and began lapping away at Liam's testicles. He strummed Liam's perineum with his fingers, sending pulse after pulse through Liam's pelvis. The sensation in Liam's stomach tightened as the arousal mounted.

'Oh my god, Julian, just take me!'

Julian said nothing. He spit onto his fingers and inserted two into Liam's rectum, curving his fingers downward just enough. Liam cried out as his lover's fingers hit a spot that made the heat rise throughout his entire body. Julian then took Liam in his mouth, engulfing his entire cock deep into his throat.

Liam shouted, arching his back and grabbing the bed sheets tightly. Sweat beaded on his forehead as he began to pant more heavily.

Julian sucked slowly at first before picking up speed – Liam thrust his pelvis upwards. Julian's finger's danced inside of his hole, as his tongue lapped away at his shaft and his mouth slid up and down the entire length of his cock.

Liam sat himself up, grabbing onto Julian's hair, pushing him to suck faster. Liam felt his lover's warm tears on his pelvis as the other vampire continued to mount his momentum.

Just when Liam thought he was going to explode, Julian pulled away. He stared up into Liam's face, and Liam knew what he wanted, he knew what he needed, just like he had said, like the very first time they made love.

Liam gently placed his hand under Julian's chin and bent to meet his lips. They kissed ardently for a few minutes before Liam rose to his knees. He pulled Julian towards him and Julian walked on his knees towards the end of the bed.

Grabbing hold of the bed board at the foot of the bed, Julian bent forward to present his perfectly smooth ass to Liam.

The excitement made Liam also feel a pang of fear at the future that lay before them both. He growled in his throat and bent quickly, nibbling his lover's ass. Liam licked Julian's perineum from behind, licking up until he reached his anus. His tongue spit saliva into his hole as he continued to devour his man's ass.

Julian groaned. Liam placed his fingers to tickle the man's balls, massaging as he slobbered all over him. Then he lifted his face, kissing Julian's back all the way up to his neck. Julian tilted his head to allow Liam to suck in some skin. Liam glided his canines gently as he aligned his ready-to-explode cock with Julian's anus.

Liam slid inside him as he nibbled Julian's neck. Julian let out a cry, and Liam saw the glint of his tears on his face illuminated by the moonlight. Liam cried out as he reached deep inside his lover's hole.

Liam grabbed Julian's cock with his hand, resting his face in his neck, and thrust back and forth. Julian bucked, adding to the pulses, all while Liam stroked him. As the elation mounted inside of him, Liam's tears continued to flow freely. He pumped Julian hard and fast, thrusting hard and fast. Julian tilted his head back, his muscles flexing as he held onto the bed board tightly, and leaned back, shouting out towards the window, canines and pale blue eyes glinting in the moonlight.

Both continued to go faster and harder until both were screaming. Julian sprayed everywhere onto himself and the bed as Liam exploded inside his anus. The orgasm continued to mount and the two vampires continued to scream.

'Julian!'

'Liam!'

And then it peaked and Liam cried out a final time before burying his face in Julian's neck to weep. He heaved and kissed his lover's nape.

'Julian,' he whispered. 'I don't want to lose you.'

He slowly slid out of him. Julian turned his face to meet Liam's mouth with a searing kiss that tingled Liam's senses. Julian pulled away, sobbing. 'I'm so scared, Liam. I want to be able to promise you forever.'

Julian turned to face Liam completely, both of them still on their knees, and they continued to make out and sob as they held each other for the rest of the night.

CHAPTER THIRTEEN

Julian arrived at the location Mandy had told him to meet her deep in the woods. He noted how this safehouse was remote enough to stage a coup without the locals knowing anything was going down, but close enough to the city to call in troops and backup.

Julian entered the stone cabin and Mandy shot to her feet, rushing to his side.

'Julian!' She hugged him.

'I'm glad to see you're okay,' Julian lied. He could sense Mandy's relief – if he had to wager a guess, it would be because it wasn't Chad walking in through that door.

'What's wrong?' Mandy could tell something was off, Julian was certain of it, but he knew how to play that into his story.

He passed a hand through his hair. 'Mandy, things are bad. I think Chad's been compromised; he's literally in bed with a werewolf.'

He closed his eyes, thinking of Liam, how they'd made love last night, and it pained him to feel the fear he felt. He knew Mandy wouldn't attack him now, she was too calculated to risk making a move when he was still too alert.

'I think Liam regrets it,' he whispered. A tear ran down his cheek. 'He regrets becoming a vampire. He regrets the whole thing.' Julian opened his eyes. 'He told me I should have let him die that night.'

Mandy put a hand to her mouth. Julian knew she was feigning sympathy. She was good, though, he'd give her that.

'I'm so scared, Mandy. I think he wants to leave me.'

* * *

Liam pressed his lips together, pained at hearing Julian say those words.

After their last night and day together, he snuck out after Julian and followed him – at a distance as to avoid detection. Now he stood several feet from the safe-house, using his vampire abilities to hear what was being said inside.

'Oh, Julian,' whispered Liam. He ensured his heart rate was still slowed – he wouldn't want Mandy or Julian to perceive him.

Upon hearing Julian lament some more to Mandy, Liam felt a pang in his heart, even if he was aware Julian knew it was not true, even if they had reconciled their grievances following their quarrel.

Liam heard a new sound, the sound of creeping humans and whispered orders. Liam turned away from the safehouse to investigate. Julian was the bait, and the vampires and werewolves were nearby, but since Mandy would have perceived the rest of them if they all arrived with Julian, they were to give him a head start, as far as Liam knew.

Liam realised Mandy would not be calling on backup – the backup was already here, which meant the vampires and werewolves were one step behind.

Liam saw his quarry: a troop of fully armed and padded cops in black gear with helmets. Liam leapt up, landing on the branch of a tall tree. He took a small rock and threw it close to the troops before disappearing from sight.

Someone in the line of troops made a signal and two soldiers broke off formation to investigate the noise. Liam waited until they were removed enough from their group.

Noiselessly, Liam dropped from the tree and landed directly behind the two soldiers. With vampiric speed, he put a hand on each of their mouths and twisted their heads outwards – their necks snapped and they fell dead.

Liam quickly stripped them both of their gear and donned the man's armour. Then he tore off their limbs and scattered them about the small area to make it look ritualistic. The blood-drenched snow was a poor imitation of the carnage these human monsters had created at the mansion, but it would do.

Weapon in hand, Liam returned to the larger group that continued to slowly edge towards the safehouse, still a short distance away. He identified the commanding officer who'd given the order before and marched up to him.

'Sir, we have a situation,' he said, his voice pitched lower than his usual timbre. He motioned with his head.

The other man nodded and walked up to a tall man in special gear. Liam realised Deputy Chief Anthony Whitlock was here. This meant there were many more forces on the way or not far – the assault was going to be bloody. Liam quelled his racing heart.

'We have a situation,' the commanding officer told Whitlock in a low voice, 'I'm taking a team to investigate.'

'Take care of it!'

'Understood.'

A group of ten soldiers followed Liam to the two dead and torn bodies – at least that was that many less who would attack Julian.

'Oh, my god!' one of them gasped.

Liam took a few more steps forward, ensuring everyone was behind him. He squared his shoulders.

'What did this?' another soldier asked, shocked.

Letting his eyes flare and his canines extend, Liam grinned sinisterly and turned to face the group. 'Me!'

* * *

'We're going to get through this, Julian,' Mandy reassured him.

'I know we will,' replied Julian.

He was waiting for an opening to reach into his coat and grab the stake he'd brought. He just needed Mandy to turn his back to him. Perhaps he'd been foolish in hoping this was going to be easy.

Mandy took a few steps towards the window, always keeping her eyes on Julian, smiling in her usual manner. She tucked a strand of auburn hair behind her ear, pressing on her earlobe ever so subtly but Julian caught it.

Julian's stomach dropped.

She knew.

Not once had she turned away from him or let her guard down. Not only that but she was acting like she was waiting for the others to come to her.

Mandy sighed. 'All right, Julian,' her tone was more grave. 'Let's cut the bullshit. I know why you're here.'

Julian studied her carefully. 'What do you mean?'

'Really? You're going to feign ignorance? I saw your expression change just now.'

'I told you why I was here, Mandy,' said Julian, 'what else would I be here for?'

Mandy pouted. 'Oh, Julian,' she derided, 'still trying to find his opening.' She laughed mirthlessly. 'The protocol always is, always has been, for as long as I've been a vampire, the elders have you come to them in situations like this. They send word and then you go to them. No one comes to you to wait. And with the tech we've got today, you're not a messenger.'

The gig was up. Julian's heart began to pound as he stared at Mandy.

She folded her arms. 'I also know what Wilbur's speciality is and the training he does, the training I know you received. You think you can penetrate my heart's natural vampiric defences? Tsss. You're still too fresh a vampire to be the one sent to kill me – plausibly. They'd assume I'd think an older vampire would be the one to do it, not you, so they assumed I wouldn't suspect you. But I suppose you were the only one it made sense to send to meet with me, except for Chad. I guess he can't face me, can he?'

'Can you blame him?!' demanded Julian.

'And there he is, the real Julian Lallard, now glaring at me,' sneered Mandy.

'Why, Mandy? Why'd you do it?' shouted Julian.

'I've been preparing for this for so long, you have no idea. Now we had the best chances of doing it,' she replied coldly.

'Because of you, Zack and Zanitha are dead.'

'And countless others too,' Mandy added nonchalantly.

'Why?' growled Julian.

'Because I never wanted this!' Her voice was harsh and shrill. 'I didn't choose it. It was forced upon me by disgusting monsters. I loathe all vampires!' she shouted. 'I am disgusted with myself every moment I exist! And everyone will pay for it. Every one of you!'

Julian instinctively side-stepped as Mandy dashed at him – and she bashed into the stone wall. He grabbed her from behind and forcefully slammed her head into the stones. Mandy bared her fangs at him, somersaulting off the wall and landing behind him. She reached for his neck but Julian flipped her forward before she could snap it. Mandy landed on the floor with a loud thud.

With supernatural speed, Julian reached into his jacket, retrieved the stake and slammed it down hard. Mandy rolled aside just as the stake struck the floor where she had been. She sprang to her feet and kicked the stake out of Julian's grip and across the room where it clattered against the wall.

She launched another attack on Julian with her long, finely manicured nails. Julian grabbed her arm and twisted. Mandy yelped and yanked, taking Julian by surprise. She came down on his arm, hissing menacingly, but he pulled free just in time.

Circling each other predatorily, eyes flared, the two bared their fangs, snarling, ready to continue their duel.

* * *

Liam swung the sniper rifle around, gripping the barrel tightly and slamming it into the soldier's face with such force it broke through flesh and bone, coming out the back of her head with a sickening squidge. Another soldier came at him and Liam leapt up, landing behind him. He punched through his back, sending guts onto the snow.

He batted away a silver knife with his bare hand, astonished that all he felt was a cold sensation. He could practically see the sparkle of the silver gunpowder on the weapons, and yet, for a reason he couldn't explain – like when Conrad Cromwell had pointed his gun at his head and pressed the silver knife to his throat – the only sensation the metal's touch did to him was a cold jolt that Liam could quickly quell.

His hyperfocus on the silver allowed him to dodge and counter-attack without fear of infection by the poison that silver was to vampires.

Baring his fangs, Liam dug into the neck of another soldier, tearing flesh and ligaments out before Liam snapped his arms out at two more humans. He pulled them towards him and bashed them together so hard, their heads caved into each other.

The raw rage and feral instinct that pulsed through Liam, the savage protectiveness urging him to keep Julian safe, and the adrenalised fear that pumped his blood, allowed him to act on reflex and basic instinct. He just knew what to do and how to do it, and he did it quietly, no matter how much he wanted to roar into the night.

Before long, the group was downed.

Wiping spatter off his face, Liam picked up a sniper rifle. Despite having no training whatsoever, he positioned himself, trusting his vampiric intuition, and took aim at one troop member. With a steady hand, he pulled back the safety catch, its soft click barely audible.

He pulled the trigger.

He watched with vampiric sight as the bullet silently whizzed towards the soldier.

Down without a sound.

Liam aimed again, and again. Two more went down – three – four.

Soldiers were now aware that someone was sniping the troops, and Whitlock went to hide in his protected vehicle.

Liam moved back, leaning against a tree, as those from the squad began searching for him. He continued to take them out, impressed with his newfound abilities. When he ran out of bullets, he leapt up a tree and remained silent and out of sight while the troops continued their search, their larger squad down by a quarter now. Liam knew more would soon arrive, but at least he'd taken out a good chunk – he'd given Julian a greater fighting chance.

A pang hit his heart, squeezing his stomach. *Julian!* Liam bounded to another tree and silently made his way towards the safehouse.

* * *

Falling flat onto his stomach, Julian cried out in pain as Mandy slammed her boot down on his hand hard, yanking his other arm back and nearly dislodging it out of its socket. Julian had to force against the movement to keep her from tearing his limb off.

He rolled onto his back and delivered a powerful blow with his boot to her stomach. Mandy staggered back. She grabbed the stake from the corner and slashed at Julian. He jumped back. She swiped diagonally and the stake cut Julian's cheek. He cried out but felt the wound heal itself almost instantly.

Mandy smashed down aggressively, holding the stake levelled with Julian's heart. Julian grabbed its shaft with his hands, forcing with all his strength to stop it as it inched closer to his heart. He jabbed his knee upwards, and again the stake went skittering across the room.

Shrieking in anger, Mandy pulled out a long thin dagger from inside her jacket. Its sleek blade was unmistakably silver. Mandy gripped the leatherbound hilt tightly with both hands.

'You leave me no choice but to resort to more dangerous means,' she growled at him.

Julian leapt out of the way as Mandy lunged towards him with the silver dagger. It came awfully close to his face. Julian lifted his arm to block the blade and bat it away as it came down towards his head.

While Mandy's attacks became desperate and aggressive, Julian's became frantic. He dropped low to avoid the blade, only to be met with a kick in the stomach as he rose, and his stomach lurched from pain, making him gag momentarily.

Mandy turned and came at him from the side, nearly grazing him as Julian darted out of the way. Mandy was so frantic, Julian could barely predict her movements, his vampiric reflexes unable to keep up with her. She laughed maniacally, relishing in being the better-skilled vampire, the elder vampire of the two.

Julian jerked back as Mandy swiped at his mid, advancing. He tripped, falling onto his ass and skidding away from her blade.

'Shit!' he cursed, panicked.

She had backed him into a corner. The dagger came down towards his chest. Julian lifted his hand and grabbed the blade to knock it sideways and away from his body.

He screamed as the pain from touching the silver burnt him. A wound like that would take time to heal, but he rather that than the alternative. Yet, a cut too deep if left unattended could prove lethal. Julian had to be careful.

Julian made to move away from the corner, but Mandy delivered a bone-crushing kick to his face and his head bashed against the wall with a crack – he was lucky no fractures split through.

Stars danced before his eyes and his vision blurred. He wondered if Chad or any of the elders would have succeeded against Mandy's fury.

Mandy relentlessly kicked Julian again, landing hard on his arms and legs, hitting him in just the right spots on his joints, relishing in his inability to move as his limbs grew numb.

This was it – Julian had failed, and he was going to die. He thought of Liam, pictured his face, and felt a pang as the promise of the forever he so desperately wanted to make to him slipped away. Tears stung his eyes.

Mandy sneered in Julian's face, taunting him with the dagger, gliding its point along his cheek and down to his chin, down to his throat. It seared, the pain agonising, and Julian was helpless to do anything – he had been rendered incapacitated. She didn't even need to grab his arms, he simply could not move – his body felt paralysed.

Julian's head lolled from side to side as he fought against unconsciousness, grunting from the pain that kept pulsing with every beat of his heart.

Mandy murmured something inaudible, leaning in close with a malicious look, pressing the point of the dagger a bit harder. Julian felt the silver blade puncture his skin. He gritted his teeth as the poison began its infection into his veins and as a trickle of blood dripped from the wound and down the blade.

Julian's heart was a deafening beating drum, he had never felt so helpless or afraid in his entire life. He wanted to speak, he wanted so desperately to utter, 'I'm sorry, Liam.' and yet he could not bring himself to vocalise anything other than his pain.

Mandy's eyes suddenly widened as she was yanked back, and then Julian saw the stake protrude from her chest as she was impaled from behind. The dagger clattered to the floor and Liam appeared behind Mandy's shoulder, seething and baring his fangs.

'Don't you dare lay a hand on my fiancé. No one touches him but me.' His voice was rough and gruff.

Blood spilled from Mandy's chest and her pale eyes darkened as life left them. Liam pulled out the stake, thick blood dripping from it, and Mandy's body slumped to the floor before turning to ash.

Julian's heart leapt as he collected his bearing, still unable to do much else than gape at his lover, barely processing the armour he had donned.

'Liam,' he breathed with effort.

Liam stared at Julian in shock. Letting the stake clatter to the floor, he bent and took Julian's face in his hands. 'Julian, are you with me?' His eyes searched him. Julian managed a nod.

Liam placed two fingers on Julian's throat where the dagger had pressed. Agonising waves of pain continued to sear through his body. Liam's hand came up smeared with blood. Julian could feel the silver seeping into his bloodstream – he could only imagine the black tendrils that were snaking from the puncture – and if the wound was not properly disinfected, he would die.

Julian croaked, trying to speak. 'She . . . rendered . . . incapa . . . ugh.' He gave up.

'The silver will soon enter your blood, won't it?' quavered Liam. 'I have nothing to clean it.' His eyes met Julian's, and Julian recognised the fire in them with which Liam always devoured him when he desired him. 'Well, it's a good thing I'm in a sucking mood.'

Before Julian could register what he meant, Liam bent towards his throat and gently placed his lips around the puncture. They felt cool compared to the hot pain from the silver. And then Liam sucked – he sucked the silver-poisoned blood out of Julian's wound.

Instantly, Julian's vision cleared as the poison was removed, the burning subsiding as a deluge of refreshing cold replaced it. But then . . . His stomach lurched in fear – yet Liam merely continued sucking Julian's silver-infected blood, and in a strange way, Julian was aroused by the sensation.

Liam pulled away and spat the blood onto the floor, spitting several times before wiping his mouth. The puncture on Julian's throat healed.

Julian stared at him, eyes wide, a mix of relief and fear staggering his heart.

Liam spat again, nearly gagging. 'No one told me silver tasted like rotten sardines,' he complained.

Julian's mouth fell open as Liam used his saliva to clean his mouth before spitting some more. He wiped his mouth once more with the back of his hand.

'So what happens if I swallow some of it?' inquired Liam, looking like a bunch of afterthoughts were racing through his mind.

'You saved my life!'

Liam smiled tenderly. 'I still owed you one.' Julian knew he was trying to be brave, but he could see the sparkle of tears in his fiancé's eyes.

Julian leapt forward and wrapped his arms around Liam, clutching him fiercely, unwilling to release.

He pulled away to look at his face. 'I think you'd have already puked out your guts had you swallowed the silver.'

Liam nodded carefully. He smacked his lips. 'Then it should be safe to kiss you, right?'

Julian let out a small laugh. Liam fervently met Julian's lips with a kiss that was warm and tender. Julian's tongue twined with Liam's, flicking up and down, frantically sparring with the other tongue.

Chuckling in relief, they pulled away. 'You definitely don't taste like rotten sardines,' Julian confirmed.

Liam laughed before a sob escaped his mouth and Julian was also overwhelmed with grief as the adrenaline came crashing down.

'I couldn't bear to remain with the others,' wept Liam. 'I couldn't let you do it alone, Julian – I just couldn't. We promised each other eternity. I had to make sure we could live it together.'

Julian's mouth crashed against Liam's lips again, and they kissed passionately, tears pouring from their eyes – now the only sensation scorching through Julian's body was the passion of his love for Liam. Leaning their foreheads together and holding each other's faces, they both laughed through their tears.

'Promise me no more life-threatening missions for a while. I need my future husband.'

Julian smiled at his fiancé. 'I promise.'

Julian and Liam heard the gunfire before the bullets reached the safehouse. Julian had figured it would only be a matter of time before the troops shot at them.

As if moving in slow motion, Julian reached for Liam's hand just as his lover reached for his. Together they lunged to the ground as silver bullets whizzed past their heads, a hair away from where they had just been. They slid across the floor, flattening themselves.

At least now, if Julian was going to die, he was going to die with the man to whom he'd promised eternity. He hoped they would reach that eternity, but if not, at least they would die together.

Liam stared at him, eyes wide and twinkling with tears. He pressed his lips to Julian's in a searing kiss as bullets continued to whip past them. One bullet ricocheted near Julian; he quickly moved his hand away. Liam placed himself over Julian and wrapped his arms around him, shielding him as bullets fell on him and bounced off him.

Julian stared in awe as some of the ricocheting silver bullets hit Liam on the head or in the face, whizzing past his bare skin, but they did nothing to him, nothing at all.

Then everything stopped.

Before the squad could reload, Liam's hand locked onto Julian's, gripping firmly, and together they dashed with vampiric speed. It was almost like the night Julian had returned to him, the night he turned Liam into a vampire, except this time, it was Liam with the quicker instincts, as though he knew where the next bullets would land and how to avoid them.

He was beautiful, with canines extended and parted lips, eyes flared so bright, his pupils were just as green and vivid as his irises, and Julian had never been more in love with him than now.

Julian felt a pang in his heart when he heard a bullet hit flesh, and he looked at the man he loved who had just been hit with a silver bullet. Liam gritted his teeth and simply kept on running, guiding Julian towards the treeline where they saw their approaching allies.

Another bullet hit Liam in the leg. He staggered momentarily but kept on running, never breaking stride.

His green eyes flashing, Liam wrapped his arms protectively around Julian as they sprinted. Another silver bullet hit his shoulder. He cried out, grunting in pain as he pressed forward, his jaw set. In that moment, Liam looked not like a vampire to Julian, but like a god.

Finally, they reached the army of vampires and werewolves, panting. Julian was shaking with fear as he looked at Liam, who stood breathing heavily and gruffly, shoulders hunched.

The vampire elders leading the force of beings stared agape at Liam.

Liam was trembling. It was not unlike the trembling Julian had witnessed from his lover when he turned him.

Liam stared at the wound in his shoulder. 'How am I still conscious?' His eyes met Julian's. 'The bullet that hit you knocked you out cold.' Liam resumed gaping at himself. 'How am I still *alive*?'

As Julian stared at Liam, the silver bullet from the other vampire's shoulder was pushed out – much like the bullet in his stomach had – and the wound stopped bleeding. The other wounds acted in the same manner, spitting out the silver bullets and healing intrinsically – and that, even faster than any regular wound normally would for a vampire.

Chad uttered something in an ancient language Julian guessed was Latin.

'What now?' asked Liam.

Chad walked to Liam, eyes wide in amazement. 'I had my suspicions when I saw you kill those guys who shot Julian, as though you just knew how, but I wasn't certain. And then again when you kissed Julian while he healed and it eased him instantly. Now I know for certain.'

'What do you know for certain?' Liam asked carefully.

'You're a *Sui Generis Lamia*, it's Latin for . . .' Chad spat a laugh. He grabbed Liam's face between his fingers, turning his head from side to side. 'Liam, you're one of the rare breeds, created only under very unique and special conditions.' He stepped back, placing his hands on Liam's shoulder, studying the healed area.

'I still don't understand what's happening to me,' admitted Liam.

'I echo that sentiment.' Julian's heart was pounding, and aching, but then . . . he realised . . . 'Fuck,' he breathed, 'something isn't happening to you, Liam, something already *has* happened to you.'

'Liam,' said Wilbur, stepping forward, 'you're immune to silver.'

Julian gaped at Liam in breathless awe. He absently put a hand to his throat. 'That's how you saved me from the puncture.' He and Liam stared at each other slack-jawed before they both broke into a grin.

'Wait, say that again? How?' Liam looked bewildered with himself.

'You were turned when you were on the brink of death, yes?' asked Chad. Liam confirmed. 'And you had metal inside of your body when you were turned, yes?' Again Liam and Julian confirmed. 'Something to do with a combination of D.N.A. and blood type, and then these circumstances that you fit into.'

Chad laughed again, whooping, and clapped Liam on the shoulder. 'Liam, my friend, there has not been a *Sui Generis Lamia* in over a thousand years. The last one was a fae, the one before, a werewolf. The very first was a woman, hence the *Lămĭa* in the title.' He shook his head in disbelief, chuckling. 'And you, my friend, are one hell of a special vampire with very special abilities.'

Julian saw Liam take it all in. 'That . . . actually explains a lot,' voiced Liam. He laughed again as the vampires rejoiced.

'And you should also possess some very unique healing abilities when it comes to saving others from silver,' added Stella, nodding in confirmation to Julian.

Liam and Julian whirled their heads towards each other. Julian stared at Liam, mouth agog and amazed by how this gorgeous man was *his* special vampire. He cupped Liam's face. 'My special fiancé.' He could hardly contain his joy and wonderment. 'And I'm the one who turned you.'

'Makes our bond all the more special,' agreed Liam, smiling sweetly. He self-consciously cleared his throat as he and Julian turned back to the others. 'Sorry.'

'No worries,' said Wilbur.

They all took another quiet moment to take in the fact that Liam was a vampire immune to silver and capable of healing beings who had silver poisoning. Then, everyone sobered.

Chad looked from Liam to Julian, drawing a deep breath and steeling himself. 'Mandy?'

'Dead,' stated Julian.

Sorrow flashed through Chad's features before being replaced by resolve. He took a step towards Julian and placed a hand on his arm. 'Thank you. *I* wouldn't have been able to do it. Thank you for risking your life to get it done.'

'Actually, it was Liam who killed her,' corrected Julian. Again everyone turned to stare at Liam in awe. 'She had me cornered and incapacitated. I couldn't move, I was fighting against unconsciousness. Liam just came in and . . .' Julian beamed at Liam. 'The man I love saved my life.'

'Just one more battle before we can actually have our eternity,' said Liam, his smile never faltering.

James cracked his knuckles and moved his head from side to side, making his neck crack and his veins stick out in a way that was as endearing as it was intimidating. 'We're itching to kill some mortals who want us dead.'

'Then let's get them,' snarled Adrienne.

* * *

Vampires and werewolves emerged from the tree-line into sight of the humans afar before retreating back as fire erupted from weapons, silver bullets raining down over them. They shielded themselves from the onslaught and continued a slow advance-retreat until few ranged weapons could continue.

Now forced to resort to melee, the humans wielded batons, knives and daggers – all pure silver – but the vampires and werewolves had fought countless wars prior and were prepared to counter any attack and protect themselves from the alloy that was their poison.

'Now, the real fun begins!' James growled with excitement.

As humans charged forward, werewolves bounded on all fours, extending their claws, their teeth becoming sharp. Even though they retained their human form, an untamed quintessence radiated their primal grace from within.

They roared as they clamoured through the humans, ripping them to shreds and drawing in feral dominance to bend the weapons if they could, rendering these inoperable.

Vampires extended canines and hissed sharply, speeding past the werewolves. Piercing the night with shrill cries, they tore their enemies limb from limb, unfurling a carpet of blood over the snow.

Their sanguine impetus was at once raw as it was refined.

Eyes paled and flared in the night, as the beings from the Underworld banded together, their millennia-old feud cast aside to eliminate their immediate foe. They continued to advance on the humans, now fewer in number, the Underworlders suffering far fewer losses than they had feared.

Liam sped from friend to friend, ally to ally, shielding them and taking hits from silver weapons for them. When a vampire or werewolf fell from silver poisoning, he dashed to them, sucking out the silver from their blood, careful to only heal, mitigating losses and saving many lives.

Finally, the humans ran out of ammo. Everything grew quiet as the last click of a gun carried on the wind.

* * *

The vampires and werewolves formed a line, with Chad and James in the lead. They marched towards the troops who were now out of ammo.

Liam marched beside Julian; Wilbur and Stella were to either side of them. Adrienne and Martin now joined them, roaring and baring their teeth, claws out. Their eyes glowed with a pure rage that showed how formidable the Sharpe Alphas were.

'Now, Stella,' began Wilbur, 'if my count totals more kills than yours, will you finally agree to go to dinner with me?'

'Still trying to woo her?' Chad inquired.

'What's this?' asked Liam.

'Wilbur's been trying to woo Stella for centuries,' explained Chad, as they all continued to march towards the nervous-looking mortals. 'And it's not that she's not interested, it's a promise they made to each other a long time ago and Wilbur hasn't relented or given up on keeping it.'

'I am a man of my word,' insisted Wilbur.

'Then I hope you are prepared to have a higher kill count than me,' replied Stella. 'If the fight ends now, however . . .'

They stopped just short of the humans. Chad stepped forward, his expression growing serious.

'Step down and there will be no need for further bloodshed,' he called out.

Anthony Whitlock strode straight towards them, seething and glaring into Chad's face.

'Which one of you demonspawn killed her!' he sputtered angrily.

'Demonspawn, it's been a while since I've heard *that* one,' James muttered.

Chad's face contorted in disdain. 'She deserved her death.' His hands balled into fists, ready to strike the man.

A little ways up, the cabin in which it had gone down between Julian, Liam and Mandy soared up into flames, the fire rising towards the soon-to-be dawn sky.

Anger raged on Whitlock's face. 'I'll make you pay for this! You'll burn in hell for burning her corpse.'

'She's already ash!' Liam snarled, as more cars pulled up on the scene and someone slammed a door hard. 'She turned to it when I drove a stake through her heart.'

'Why you!' Whitlock lifted his arm high, a silver knife gleaming in his hand.

'Put the weapon down, Whitlock'

Anthony Whitlock froze at the command and slowly turned his head, careful to keep his weapon levelled. 'Mayor Hayes! Chief of Police Cheng?'

The Mayor stood with a contingent of officers, non-silver weapons pointed at Whitlock and his troops. Beside him stood a woman with a glare intimidating enough to make anyone cower.

'What *is* this?' Hayes admonished. 'Killing innocent people. Just because this is right outside of town, doesn't make it right. These are my townsfolk. This is *my* city and you're still in it.'

'These people are criminals! Monsters!' growled Whitlock. The troops who now had their rifles and guns trained on the D.C. remained vigilant.

'What is the crime?' Cheng demanded. 'I see your troops with weapons and people dead. I also recognise the Cromwell mobsters among your troops. This gives me no other choice than to arrest you for conspiring with and engaging in criminal acts with a dangerous crime syndicate.'

'Wait! No! These are vampires and werewolves!' cried Whitlock, lowering his arm.

Mitchell Hayes bellowed a laugh. 'Surely you don't believe that!'

'And besides, how are you even here? Why are you here?' demanded Whitlock.

'We got a call from an informant,' replied Hayes, 'and Cheng put her best people on it.' He stepped towards Whitlock. 'I finally get to catch you in nefarious acts after all these years and get your ass arrested.'

'You don't believe me, do you?' Whitlock nodded dangerously. 'I'll prove it.'

In one swift motion, he jabbed Liam, who instinctively turned sideways. The knife slid in through his ribs and blood began to drench his clothes. The wound wasn't deep but the pain was a real bitch and Liam shouted out through gritted teeth.

'Whitlock! Have you lost your goddamn mind!' bellowed Hayes, grabbing Whitlock by his collar and yanking him away from Liam.

Liam put a hand to his still bleeding wound. Again, the sensation he felt was pure cold, like ice sticking to his skin, but it was already subsiding and he knew the cut would heal itself within moments. Had it been anyone else, their skin would already be snaking out with inky tendrils and they'd be out cold if not already dead.

'Now you've really gone and done it!' Hayes shouted angrily.

Whitlock stared at Liam, mortified, and Liam stared at him, eyes just as wide. Liam looked down at his wound. Inside he could feel it mend. Outside, it still looked fresh, but even with the seconds that passed, the blood had ceased seeping out.

'Clearly, this young man is no vampire or werewolf. Honestly, where do you hear these things?' Chief of Police Cheng signalled her troops and they advanced on Whitlock and cuffed him. 'You're under arrest.'

An officer recited Whitlock's rights as he was taken away, Cheng followed close behind, issuing orders to more of her troops.

Hayes looked at Liam, confused and concerned. 'Are you all right? I'm terribly sorry, but then again,' he lowered his voice, 'better you than your friends. I seriously thought you were one of them, I would have hated for any more of you to die tonight. Sorry I arrived later than planned. Cheng likes to do things by the book, and, seeing as she doesn't know about you all . . .'

'Uh, it's all right.' Liam hesitated.

Adrienne and Martin were quick to walk to the Mayor's side as Cheng's officers were already filling out notes for their reports on what they had seen here tonight. None reported any vampires or werewolves, only mobsters, and Anthony Whitlock being part of them. All of Whitlock's troops were arrested or taken down if they fought back.

Wilbur was now giving a statement to one of the officers – he had previously declared he would risk daylight if one of them had to. He had a stronger tolerance than most anyway, but Stella was by his side, answering questions, as well as moving things along so they could wrap everything up before the sun rose.

Mayor Hayes continued to scowl in concern at Liam, eyeing his wound.

'Are you sure you don't need a medic?' asked Hayes.

Liam leaned towards the mayor, suppressing a laugh, and angled himself so only Hayes would see his face. 'I'm one of the special ones.' He flashed him a grin, fangs glinting in the moonlight.

Hayes cocked a brow up. 'Well then, good job.' He turned to Adrienne. 'And the prime suspect working with Whitlock?'

'She was taken out by one of our own. We're burning the evidence.' Adrienne glanced at Liam, winking. Liam smiled, taking that in – the Alpha of a werewolf pack had just called a vampire one of their own. He was pleased as a warm sensation of appreciation filled his heart.

Julian took Liam's hand in his and led him away from all the troops and commotion. Liam sighed, looking down, though not at his healed wound but at the dagger in its sheath at his belt.

'You kept her dagger?' gasped Julian.

'I'm immune,' Liam protested, lifting his shoulders for a few seconds and meeting Julian's beautiful gaze. He relaxed his shoulders. 'I feel I should keep it. Someone who can handle silver should. Plus, it makes me look less like a typical vampire.'

Julian breathed out a small laugh. 'I love you, Liam.'

Liam smiled at him, biting his lower lip. 'I love you, Julian.'

'Let's not wait.' Julian held Liam's hand and gently rubbed his thumb on his ring finger. He stopped at the ring. 'Let's do it as soon as we can.'

'I can't wait to call you my husband,' whispered Liam. Julian beamed at him.

Liam's focus shifted to Chad and James, who were fussing over each other, and he and Julian looked over at them.

'My pack will just have no choice but to accept that their future Alpha is with a vampire,' insisted James. 'I'm ready to leave the pack for you. Chad, baby . . . I'm not losing you. I know what I feel.' He took Chad's hand and placed it on his heart. 'I'm not going to let the wars of our ancestors keep us apart.'

'That's actually really romantic, you know that?' Chad's lips curled into a smile on the side of his mouth. His face grew serious again. 'Everything that's happened made me realise that I won't let anything keep us apart either. Whatever happens, it happens to us together. I love you, James.'

'I love you, Chad.'

The two men kissed, their passion growing by the minute.

'I think it's their turn to need us to vacate the premises and let them have their moment after a battle,' Julian whispered in Liam's ear.

The way he said it, and the sheer memory of that time, sent a shiver through Liam's body and his heart racing. He bit his lower lip, turning to face Julian.

'Maybe we could find our own spot as well,' he suggested.

They chuckled, sighing in relief.

'It's finally over, perhaps now things can calm down, just a little bit?' pondered Liam.

He and Julian stared at each other for a moment, assessing that thought, then burst out laughing. 'No chance!'

Epilogue

Liam looked down at his trembling hands and shook them again. He felt like his heart was going to beat right out of his chest.

'How can my heart beat so fast when I'm a vampire?! I thought being immortal meant I could control it better.'

'Don't ask me!' protested Rachel. 'I'm not the immortal being with the special gifts here. Just calm down, everything's going to be fine.' She fixed the collar of Liam's tuxedo. 'This is the moment you've dreamt of for months!'

Liam felt sweat drip down his back. He was shaking like he'd never shaken before. He was so nervous.

'I'm gonna puke.'

'Relax, Liam, this is your big day!'

Rachel placed her hands firmly on his shoulders and peered into his eyes. 'I love you.' She smiled.

'You're all the family I will ever need. I'm so proud of you.'

Liam's eyes filled with tears. 'Oh my god, Rachel! Stop being so sappy.'

The music began and Liam breathed in sharply. 'Why am I so goddamn scared right now!'

'Because you're about to get married to the man of your dreams and spend all of eternity with him – literally. You're both immortal beings. Now's the time to back out if that's what you want.'

Liam knew she was only teasing and it calmed his nerves. He wanted this.

Again he looked down at his hand devoid of his ring. Ever since Julian had given him the golden band, they had both worn them constantly, but for today, they removed them, because these were also their wedding rings.

Rachel presented her arm to Liam. 'You ready?'

Liam nodded. 'I'm ready.'

He looped his arm through hers and together they walked down the aisle to where Julian stood waiting, handsome as ever, his blue eyes shining. He looked just as nervous as Liam felt, and Liam could hear his lover's heartbeat pumping just as quickly as his own.

Liam came to stand before him and they took hold of each other's hands.

Wilbur was officiating and he spoke a few eloquent words.

And then Wilbur asked them to speak their vows.

'Liam,' began Julian, sobbing through his speech, 'when I met you, I knew right away that I loved you, and I soon realised I would love you for all eternity. It makes me so happy that you are with me, part of my life, part of me, and that you are what I am – that you embrace with such devotion our new life as you embrace me with such passion.

'You are the first human I've ever turned, and that makes our bond all the more special to me. I promise to love you for as long as my eternal life continues. I promise to make you the happiest man alive. I love you so much, words cannot express it. Liam . . .' Julian paused. 'I love you with all my heart. I will love you eternally.'

Liam blinked as tears poured down his face. Julian was so handsome as he wept in joy before him.

'Julian, from the moment I looked into your eyes I knew you would be special to me. When my life flashed before me and I was offered the choice to become a vampire and be eternal with you, I knew the answer without having to think about it, because I knew *then* I wanted to devote my life to you, and for that, I had to be alive.

'I will spend all of eternity showing you all of my love. You saved my life, and then I saved yours.' Liam's vision blurred as more tears poured from his eyes; he struggled through the rest of his sobbing speech, trying to remain as coherent as he could. 'You asked me if what I said was a proposal, and we sealed our fate. You make me so happy, Julian. I will gladly spend forever with you.'

Julian laughed tearfully, squeezing Liam's hands. Rachel blew her nose, as did Chad who was sitting next to her.

Then came time for the rings, brought by Chad who presented them on a pillow with a flourish. He beamed at them, his eyes twinkling. Liam and Julian each took the other's ring before simultaneously sliding them onto their fingers. It felt nice to have the golden band back on.

'Julian, Liam, do you take each other for all eternity?'

'I do!' asserted Julian.

'I do!' declared Liam.

'Then I now pronounce you, vampire husbands!'

Cheers erupted as Julian pounced onto Liam for a searing kiss. And again they sob-laughed their joy.

* * *

Chad had bawled through his speech as Julian's best man. To think how they had grown so much closer in the past months – and Chad had delivered one fine speech. Wilbur, Stella, Adrienne and Martin's speeches had been more composed. They had said a few quick words before the main speeches of the night, which followed a grand meal in a lavish mansion they had selected for the occasion of this midnight wedding.

Now it was Rachel's turn to speak.

'Liam,' she wept, breathing heavily into the microphone, 'I am *so* proud of you. When we left home together, I promised you I'd always look out for you and be there for you. You might have special powers now, but I know you'll always need me, and I will always need you. You're all the family I need, Liam. I'll be looking out for another one soon,' she rubbed her belly, 'but I will always be your big sister. I'll always be here for you, for as long as my mortal life continues.'

She glanced at all the attendees. 'I never thought I'd be standing here with vampires and werewolves, but you always said you'd have an unusually spectacular wedding someday. You weren't wrong!'

There were laughs from the guests.

'I guess what I'm trying to say – as I'm babbling on – is that I love you, you'll always be my little brother, and I'm so happy for you.'

Liam hugged Rachel. 'I love you too, Rachel. I always will, my sister.'

Liam pulled away, and before Rachel could sit, Keisuke stood, taking the mic from her.

'I'd like to say a few words too.' He looked about nervously. 'I am honoured to have so many of you put your trust in me. I am honoured to know you and to see vampires and werewolves come together today to celebrate the love of two men whose love and devotion can only be matched by one other.' He turned to look at Rachel. 'Mine to you.'

Rachel put a hand to her mouth, looking romantically touched.

'Rachel, whatever is thrown our way, knowing you, loving you, is all I want to do.' He placed his hand on her stomach. 'We have a child on the way.

A family with you – unexpected as it was – makes me the happiest man alive.' He glanced at Liam and Julian. 'Well, perhaps one of the happiest men alive.' He chuckled nervously. 'Rachel, I promised you I would show you what it was to be loved by me.'

Keisuke knelt down on one knee. 'Every day I am more in love with you than the last. Will you do me the honour of becoming my wife? Will you marry me?'

Liam beamed at Keisuke and Rachel. Everyone grew quiet to hear Rachel's answer.

'Come on, give him the answer I know you want to say,' Liam muttered.

Rachel laughed. 'Yes! Yes, Keisuke, I will marry you!'

Everyone erupted into cheers again and Keisuke rose to kiss Rachel, long and fervently, one hand cupping her face and one on the small of her back. He pulled away tenderly, leaving Rachel blushing through her makeup.

'Anyone else want to declare their love?' asked Julian cheekily, glancing towards Chad and James.

They held up their interlaced hands. 'We already have and much more.'

'Oh-ho!'

Everyone laughed as the dancing began. Liam and Julian danced first to a soft tune, then a slow song began and couples joined them on the dance floor: Rachel and Keisuke, Chad and James, Stella and Wilbur, Adrienne and Martin.

Liam tenderly laced his arms behind Julian's neck, drawing him close and leaning his forehead against his husband's. 'Funny how I'm the one who proposed but you've taken on the role of the groom and me the bride.'

'That *is* what you wanted,' Julian reminded.

'True.' Liam's gaze fixed solely on Julian, the dancers around them blurred into insignificance. 'And what is it that you want, my husband?'

Julian smiled, radiating his love. 'Liam, my husband, what I want . . .' Biting his lip seductively, he brought his mouth to Liam's ear and whispered, 'Slip away with me.'

Their bodies moving as one, they danced towards the exit and disappeared before anyone could notice. The party would rage on without them.

Their lips were already pressed hard against each other, mouths devouring ardently and tongues twining together, when they barged into their private room. Julian pushed Liam against the door, slamming it shut.

Panting heavily, Liam parted from Julian's lips only to catch some air before plunging back in. Tugging hurriedly, he tore Julian's clothes off as Julian fumbled to undress Liam.

Julian pulled Liam closer to him and towards the bed, kissing him voraciously. He turned Liam and together they fell onto the bed, bodies flushed against each other, Julian on top of Liam. Julian licked Liam's neck, from his collarbone to his ear.

Liam moaned softly, feeling his husband's erection rub against his. Sliding up and down him, Julian's breath grew rough with desire.

'Liam, my husband,' he whispered huskily, sending a warm shiver running down Liam's neck.

'Julian,' Liam cried softly, 'my husband.'

With his elbows on either side of Liam's face, Julian continued to kiss him hungrily, and Liam felt Julian's warm fluid seep onto him – just a trickle, but it was enough to make him gasp loudly.

'Vampire husband!' declared Liam. 'I'm in a sucking mood.'

Julian grinned. Straddling Liam, Julian straightened and gently began to trace his fingers along the other man's length. Liam arched his back, feeling a tremor pulse from his pelvis.

'Oh my god, Julian, you're such a fucking tease,' Liam complained.

Julian chuckled. He began to rub Liam's moist shaft with his thumb, tracing tantalising circles, and then he took his own cock in his hands. Staring at Liam, his eyes growing dark with elation, he began to stroke himself, rubbing against Liam.

A sweet aching need surging within him, Liam reached for Julian, who, smiling tauntingly, pushed his hand away.

'Oh my god, Julian!'

'I want to hear you cry out for me,' Julian commanded. 'Tell me how much you want this cock. How much do you want my cock?'

'Julian,' Liam whimpered elatedly, 'I want you. I want to suck you. I want your cock between my canines.' He asserted more loudly, 'I want to fucking suck you – now!'

Julian let out a gruff moan in response to Liam's tone. Biting his lower lip, Julian lifted himself and turned around, presenting his ass and hard dripping cock to Liam.

Liam grabbed hold of Julian's ass, licking Julian's perineum up to his anus. He thrust his tongue into the hole and Julian moaned feverishly.

'Liam, take me!'

Liam grinned sideways, gazing down his body to where Julian was lowering himself to lick Liam's testicles.

Liam merely continued to lick his husband's balls and perineum, gliding his tongue, and then he began to suck in the skin there, jutting his tongue into Julian's ass – his tease was his sweet vengeance.

Julian took Liam into his mouth, sucking him, canines enveloping his cock and Liam shouted into Julian's rectum. His tongue danced around, as Julian sucked him harder, fingers tickling and massaging the area beneath.

Liam felt himself stiffen and Julian continued, quickening his pace, and an inebriating wave washed over him and he let it all go. Jerking his head back on the pillow, Liam screamed out into the room.

* * *

Swallowing the warm semen that gushed into his mouth, Julian pulled Liam out of him and admired his plump cock. He plunged Liam's cock back into his mouth, making him drip cum again. Julian continued to suck until he was certain there was nothing left to ejaculate . . . for now.

And then he felt two fingers enter his anus and his cock was taken into his husband's mouth, canines gliding along the length of his erection, adding to the sensation of euphoria boiling over inside of Julian.

Julian cried out and Liam continued fervently, his pace never relenting, but also never quickening. It made Julian slide up and down, wanting more friction. The room spun around him as he felt himself become dizzy with the ecstasy of his orgasm. His cock stiffened and then Julian screamed, feeling his fluid spill out in one large jet into Liam's mouth.

Liam pulled him out slowly. Julian was still panting, still hungry for more of his husband. He was so happy, so elated, he could not express it in words. He only wanted to keep devouring Liam all night.

Julian turned back around, pulling Liam to his knees and drawing his face closer to his. He parted his lips and their mouths crashed against each other with passion and hunger, a lust for each other like none other they'd ever experienced.

Without saying a word, without needing to speak, Julian turned Liam around and pushed into his rectum, gripping Liam's still-hard cock in his hands.

Breathing gruffly, Julian bucked, harder and harder, all while pumping Liam. Together they shouted louder and louder, screaming into the night long and hard, as Julian's orgasm culminated once more and he exploded into Liam who spilled onto his hand.

Laughing and panting, they fell onto the bed, kissing ferociously, and rubbing all their fluid onto each other's chests. Julian lowered himself, nibbling Liam's pecs before coming back to meet his lips.

They rubbed against each other, again and again, building up momentum once more, and again screaming long and loud, ejaculating onto and into each other, sucking each other's cocks, asses, balls, and showing each other their eternal love again and again.

Their bodies were covered in semen, sticky with sweat, and it only added to the arousal they both felt.

Julian licked Liam's balls, up his cock, to his shaft, his naval, his chest – Julian's tongue glided all the way up to Liam's mouth, never leaving his skin. Their mouths opened to engulf each other's lips, their tongue jabbed into each other's mouths. Their cocks continued to be hard, continued to spill, and when they were done, they were so hot and sweaty, but neither of them cared.

Julian held Liam tightly, intoxicated by his scent. Prompted by his husband, Julian stood and followed him to the bathroom where Liam started the shower. They rinsed off their bodies of the accumulated sweat and semen.

'We've never done this before,' began Julian, his whisper husky, 'but two vampires can drink each other's blood to satiate their need for sustenance, and it also enhances their senses and desires.' He brought his lips closer to Liam's ear, dropping his voice to a sultry level. 'Especially when it's with the one who turned you.'

Julian instantly felt Liam's heart quicken, while his own anticipation mounted.

'Show me how it's done.' Liam's voice was at once commanding and pleading, and it made Julian spasm with arousal.

Not bothering to shut the water off, Julian stepped out of the shower and, taking his husband's hand in his, pulled Liam to the fogging-up mirror.

Standing behind him, Julian gently dug his extended canines into Liam's shoulder close to his neck, and sucked on his blood. Liam let out a gentle moan, tilting his head to give Julian better access to his neck. Julian closed his lips as he drank in his lover's life source.

Julian slowly pulled out, his canines painted crimson, and he licked his lover's blood off them, savouring the way Liam tasted. Liam merely stared at Julian's reflection, his green eyes smouldering with desire.

Liam turned around to face Julian, looking ready to swallow him whole, and followed his instructions. Julian immediately felt his cock become erect again as soon as Liam's teeth grazed his neck, the small pinch as they sank in elicited a pulse inside of him.

When Liam pulled his canines out and lifted his head to look at Julian, he saw in Liam's eyes the same fire he felt as they flared and paled once more.

'Fuck!' Liam breathed.

Julian groaned, sneering his thirst. 'When I said we'd go all night, I meant it.'

Liam's lips were smudged on one side with Julian's blood and his canines were still bright and scarlet. Somehow it made him look even more deliciously handsome and sexy to Julian.

Liam moved to stand behind Julian and pressed up against him, pushing into him in one go.

Julian braced himself, placing his hand on the fogged-up mirror, mildly aware of the water that was still running from the showerhead. He could see their foggy reflections as Liam thrust deeper inside of him, pulling out ever so slightly and thrusting in deep again.

The sight of their eyes flashing, with their sharp canines glinting, their muscles flexing and tensing, and the drip of blood that trickled down Liam's canine and plopped onto Julian's shoulder sent a thrill surging through Julian's body.

Julian grabbed his own cock, stroking himself, as Liam pumped inside of him, holding onto Julian's shoulders. The droplet of blood tickled Julian's skin as it slowly oozed down his chest. It perched at his nipple, making it hard, making him breathe out a syncopated breath, and increasing his zenith.

Julian tilted his head back, feeling Liam's hot breath on his neck as the heat of their passion mounted, a sanguine sincerity so strong, only through intimate touch could it be expressed.

They screamed together, an elongated cry of euphoria, dizzy with orgasms that never relented.

At last, exhausted but elated, they moved back to the bedroom and fell onto the bed. They wrapped their arms around each other, ready to sleep together as husbands for the first time, ready to spend eternity together, ready for whatever came next. Nuzzling into each other's necks, finally feeling content and satiated, they drifted off to sleep.

<u>THANK YOU SO MUCH FOR READING!</u>

If this book was satisfying to you,
please consider taking a few moments
to write a review on Amazon or Goodreads.
It would mean so much.

Thank you.

<u>More To Come</u>

In the thrilling and sexy sequel, *Primal Passion*.

*One year after the events that saw the beginning
of the vampire-werewolf alliance,
Chad struggles to overcome his grief.
The alliance comes under threat when a mysterious
Alpha goes after James, intent on reigniting
the war between the two factions.
Borne from the events of the previous year,
an unlikely ally joins their efforts.
Yet, their abilities are tested when Chad and James
are forced to face sacrifice.*

Acknowledgements

It has been such a pleasure writing Sanguine Sincerity and developing my vampire fiancés. The novel was first a short story that later became Chapter One and then developed into an entire series of books, for which I am most excited.

So then the first person I wish to acknowledge is my friend on Medium, Christine Graves, whose publication I initially wrote Sanguine Sincerity for. That spark of inspiration brought Liam and Julian together . . . for all eternity.

All who have supported me on this journey and encouraged me helped me stay motivated. I'd gush about my characters to my husband, who'd chuckle in amusement as I'd ramble about, and in this way, I could voice ideas that allowed me to further develop the story.

I must also acknowledge my artist, Kemvee, who brought Liam and Julian to life through her art. The portraits as well as the cover are so meticulously drawn. I've worked with her before, and she always goes above and beyond my expectations. Her depiction of Liam and Julian makes me feel like I can hear them as they gaze into each other's eyes. I can hear Julian growl in his throat in anticipation, Liam moan in yearning. Truly, a sensational work of art.

And now the story doesn't reach its end here, there are many encores to come. The next instalment focuses on Chad and James, though Liam and Julian remain main characters in the series. I am eager for you to discover the primal passion shared between the unusual pair that is our ancient vampire and soon-to-be pack Alpha.

Also Published by Binky Ink

Stardust Destinies I: Variate Facing
Stardust Destinies II: The Drought
(https://binkyproductions.com/stardustdestinies)

Multiple Short Stories on Medium
Soon To Be Published in Book Format
(https://medium.com/@binkyinkwriting)

Eidahs is a pseudonym for all mature written works, from thrillers to erotic romance. Eidahs in pronunciation sounds

elven in nature, which is why she chose it, to tap into her love of fantasy, a genre that couples well with super-natural and preternatural, dark fantasy, and romance.

Eidahs is also the nickname 'Shadie' backwards, repre-senting the shadow self, innermost desires, and a spectrum of emotions, most notably, passion, sorrow, rage, and delight, which Eidahs loves to incorporate in her writing. Enticing readers and evoking the characters' emotions when she writes has guided her inspiration to spell many short stories on Medium and a series of books under this pen name.

Connect with Binky Ink:

WordPress Website & Blog
    https://binkyproductions.com/binkyinkwriting
Medium – Main Profile
    https://medium.com/@BinkyInkWriting
Medium – Erotica Fan-Fiction
    https://medium.com/erotica-fan-fiction
Medium – Dominium Tenebrarum – The Underworld
    https://medium.com/dominium-tenebrarum-the-underworld
X (Twitter) https://twitter.com/binkyinkwriting

www.ingramcontent.com/pod-product-compliance
Lightning Source LLC
Chambersburg PA
CBHW070434120726
47910CB00003B/783